// JJ'S EYES

JJ'S EYES

A Documentary

David Michaels

Copyright © 2003 by David Michaels.

ISBN: Softcover   1-4134-3604-8

All rights reserved. No part of this book may be reproduced or transmitted in any form or by any means, electronic or mechanical, including photocopying, recording, or by any information storage and retrieval system, without permission in writing from the copyright owner.

This is a work of fiction. Names, characters, places and incidents either are the product of the author's imagination or are used fictitiously, and any resemblance to any actual persons, living or dead, events, or locales is entirely coincidental.

This book was printed in the United States of America.

To order additional copies of this book, contact:
Xlibris Corporation
1-888-795-4274
www.Xlibris.com
Orders@Xlibris.com
20588

Opening Shots

We were old enough to have known better, I guess. Really, you should expect for things to turn out badly when you're almost thirty and you and some friends you've known since high school decide to meekly stave off the impending malaise of adulthood and make a documentary about James Joyce's vision problems that will prominently feature your friend's dying father, reading aloud long passages from *Ulysses*. What sort of people would think this is a good idea? Shiftless? Clueless? Dumb? Probably all of the above. Or were we really just geniuses on to something so huge that the Western world was just not ready for? Maybe, we shouldn't have expected to get rich and hang out with Matt Damon, but still . . . isn't all art born from wide-eyed optimism and that "can-do" spirit that makes us all proud to be American artists?

Fade out shot of American flag waving in the breeze.

Cue the music, "*The Star-Spangled Banner*" played by a Klezmer band, a clarinet mimicking the sound of the electric guitar feeding back.

A hand writing the titles on a handheld chalkboard:

> JJ's Eyes: A Documentary
> *(An American Film with Words)*
> A Starkweather Production
> Executive Producer: Niall Black, Esq.

The sound is thin and scratchy

A still photograph of Ezra Pound, seated at a white table at an outdoor café. He is wearing a straw hat—almost like a sombrero. His hand appears to be scratching his beard. He is smiling. It is 1932.

"It got to be I couldn't stand sitting next to him at dinner parties. The way he would slurp his soup. So damn loud, GULPING it, with an extra emphasis on the final upward rush of air against his molars. Like he was born in FRANCE. Who the hell did he think he was? He was born in Dublin, which may as well have been Detroit (a REAL AMERIKUN CITY), for its utter lack of charm and sophistication. Dublin was always a cheap, rip-off of London, just as Detroit was of Chicago, and so forth . . . If only he hadn't written all those words. Those luminescent words that glowed on the page and whose sounds would rattle about in your brain like some half-remembered villanelle or nursery rhyme sung by Li Po's mother as she washed white shirts in the cool, gentle waters of the Yangtze River three thousand years ago. Those words . . ."

(Ezra Pound writing to President Roosevelt about James Joyce. Excerpted from *The Collected Economic Insights of Ezra Pound: Towards a New Paradigm of Commerce*.)

Who among us is not Oedipus?

Perhaps, this is the question that must be asked. All wrapped up in the tragedy of our own making. Returning to gray-covered days of primitive memory. Yellowing pages at the edges. But then, all progress is yellow and grayed in tragedy, isn't it? As we roll our heads or merely, meekly, shuffling along in grimfaced deathwatch. As we save the wine and hug the sheep. Shift the swine and mugging the leap. And all good things at that.

Je suis Americaine.

Icarus flew too near the sun on waxed wings. The sun blinded the stranger. Oedipus, the lustful son, was blinded by fate—would such crimes bring more than a beep to your Blackberry? The man in *Pi* disobeyed his mother and stared into the sun and got a really big tumor and wandered around the subway in stylish black and white, with a pounding techno soundtrack. Abraham was set to kill his son out of obedience, fear and trembling indeed. Cronus ate his children for lunch, their little feet kicking as he slurped them down. Yum . . . yummy. God's son, our lord and savior, Jesus Christ, was hung on a tree in Calvary as a common criminal, where he was humiliated by thugs, before he turned over his soul to his father, thus saving us from eternal damnation. The lady down the street shot her twin sons in their heads when they were four years old. Oops. Perhaps, she was just cleaning her shotgun. What would Henry Ford say? The litany of children killed in the city of Detroit this year by their parents or of their parents, in one year alone, would neither shock nor awe, but then there it is.

The point is books are useless because they don't do anything. They don't heal, they don't touch, they don't breathe, they don't move. Anyone who said a book changed the course of human events, even the course of their exceedingly dull lives, was a liar—most likely a writer, too. A bad writer at that, "exceedingly dull," talk about overwriting. If you caught that, then please continue reading. If not, don't. Your rather puny brain would not appreciate the subtle wit and dazzling intelligence imbued in each and every phoneme, end mark, and—dare I say it?—spacing in this book. Note: if you count the number of spaces in this book and apply it to a very secret math formula—the Macgillicuddy Proof, then you will be able to build an impenetrable dollhouse—a 1:356 scale version of the Ford Fairlane Estate. In the end, books are little more than depositories of failed ambitions and anemic fantasy called words and ideas. They aren't real. They used to be just ink on parchment; now, they are bits scratched on magnetic tape or bits on a silicon chip, or even if some ink is involved, they are digitized beyond all recognition. It is likely that no human ever touched this book product until you purchased it. The writer does not count. He is not real either. He is just a character I created to avoid the toil of quotidian life—the folding of clothes, the dusting of shelves, the vacuuming of floors, the phoning of friends, and the waves to the neighbor down the street, who may or may not be a potential pedophile. The facts: a tall man, fleshy, black hair, thinning at the top. Mustache. Living with his sister and her ten-year-old son, all moving from Minneapolis (to Elkville, of all places.) Moreover, he often will play catch, Frisbee, and just "rap" (his words) with adolescent boys and girls. Then they will go in the house for a brief "lemonade" break. He does not work. He walks his nephew to the local elementary school, leaving forty-five minutes early for a ten-minute walk so he can watch his nephew play on the playground to ensure he is assimilating adequately in the local community. Of course, any discussion of this with Stephen will result in chastisement. His opprobrium of Liz and my "puritanical" and "provincial" morals never wavers. Stephen does not have children.

Regardless, it is extreme sloth that drives me to the monorail keyboard and the flickering Samtron monitor on these Saturday mornings, not a desire to communicate, illuminate, or entertain. I have nothing to say, having a dull voice with which to say it, yet am encouraged by the lack of impediment these disadvantages may cause in the literary marketplace. I have read many books on the subject of books and have consulted with several members of a local writers' club which meets at the downtown Starbucks and am convinced that I have a sound marketing plan, which I will divulge slowly throughout the course of this enterprise to prevent you from realizing what a sham this whole endeavor is, and attempting to sue me. Or when you realize how simple it all is, put the book down and write and market one yourself, leaving my book to sit idly on the shelf. Rather, in the ether of the digital void. Although, I suppose once you've paid for it and I've cashed your check, I should not care what you do with it. Still, as I am a weak-willed and vain man, who did spend a fair amount of time and underwent a moderate level of wrist pain in keying this in, I would like you to at least finish reading it. So I will dole out the goodies like a masterful pol. All politics is local, none so much so as the politics of the mind. I am not quite sure what that means, but if you don't think too much about it, it has a vaguely profound air about it. I think that advice will serve you well for the rest of this experience. If you don't expect too much, you shall not be disappointed.

If I had more friends, I'd have skipped the book and made an independent film because cinema, on the other hand, is the real deal.

The belief that we too could have attended Harvard, had we applied.

Stephen stood at the counter of Strichoff's Rare Books, on a nameless street (Charles) in a nameless city (Cambridge), where he was one of many hyper-educated book clerks, dismissed from a Harvard doctoral program unceremoniously after failing his qualifying exams. Now a master of literature, and a mister of misanthropy, mostly a miser of mild proportions, he scratched the back of his neck. His hair, for argument's sake, is reddish, but not annoyingly so. He used his right hand, the dominant one, for scratching. This of course has no bearing on the general outcome of the story, nor will it have prevented his father from dying a long and painful death to cancer. For clarity, the death was average, the suffering relatively long. Still, as my intent is to sell as many books as possible, I will attempt to include those details which readers demand: melodramatic hospital scenes, where father and son reconcile their estranged relationship; the bedroom scene, where the father has an EPIPHANY (while reading *Ulysses*), perhaps even a scene at the funeral, where the son makes a BRAVE and SWEETLY SENTIMENTAL eulogy, even, dare I say it, bagpipes, as they throw the ashes into the Atlantic Ocean off a craggy Scottish cliff? Just when you think you can't stand the pain of the beauty of heightened human suffering, the deft hand of the gentle *deus ex machina* will carry you to tender and funny scenes, where several characters engage in witty, intellectual banter and offer keen insight into contemporary social problems, including poverty and the maltreatment of children. If you don't think you can stand it, you can wait for the made-for-television movie on local access cable, for which I have received several enticing proposals.

I wish

I could touch a button and you would know everything you needed to become your own personal Stephen. It would make your life so much easier for the next two hours or so that it takes to watch this film. Or for you (enter your name here), that it takes to read this book.

Stephen looked at his watch and realized that David and Elizabeth (Liz is a spunky, diminutive derivation of Elizabeth) would not be coming to visit him from Detroit, after all. His lips turned upwards slightly in smug knowingness. He was disappointed too, but would not grant them this for more than a second. He resumed entering the new arrivals into the database. When was the last time he had seen them? Not their wedding; he was doing some research on Henry James at the National Museum in London at the time, the late 1990s, and could not afford the time and expense of international air travel. That was so long ago, even to him, even now. Five years, 18 percent of his time on this earth, at least in this life, in this corporeal entity. He had loved them both once in exactly the same way, fraternal love, never experiencing erotic attraction to either of them, an observation that struck him now as quite odd. Even David's soft brown eyes and gentle laugh, or Liz' fiery eyes and taut calf muscles had ever stirred in him anything stronger than admiration or affection. Once, on a camping trip to the Pictured Rocks National Lakeshore along the shores of bitter Lake Superior, he had observed, quite accidentally, Liz topless as she changed clothes in her tent with the rain flap unfurled, and he stood for a moment in the shadow of a birch tree and admired her ample bosom and the tight golden skin of her arms and belly, and the white mask of skin at her upper portion. Were I a painter, I should paint her, he chuckled.

The moment ended when she finished pulling her blue T-shirt, ripped at the shoulder, over her bra and glanced over towards him. He was quite confident she had not seen him standing, staring at her, until a slow smile grew upon her face, leaving him flushed red with embarrassment. In proper form, they never spoke of this moment to any other living soul.

They were supposed to be here four hours ago. They left a message yesterday saying they had arrived in Boston and would call him today, Thursday, for lunch. He hated to admit he wanted to see them desperately, even as he begrudged them their quiet middle-class, Middle Western suburban existence. He hated to admit he was homesick, ashamed he could be after almost ten years of living away. He usually only felt this way at holidays, and when the occasional friend would come to visit, with many visitors and frequently at first, fewer as time passed and people became more entrenched in their tiny universes, as promotions were received and children were conceived, and a few even entering kindergarten this fall, according to a recent letter.

David and Liz were usually a bit unreliable, but four hours late seems to be a bit much. They were ex-punk rock stars, after all, and preferred doing things **on their own terms**, even when this pissed off their own best friends. Dropping off the face of the earth for months at a time. No phone calls, no e-mail, just nothing. And then, a phone call a week ago, all pleasant and cheerful and genuine, as if they had spoken everyday over the past year, or was it longer? The good thing about David is he isn't much for chitchat on the phone—no annoying small talk. So the phone calls are usually brief and refreshing. Stephen was not one to be all uptight about Miss Manners kind of stuff, but four hours, for God's sake—a phone call would have been nice, don't you think? Maybe it was not homesickness that troubled Stephen as much as the fear of the dreadful questions asked, and the half-mumbled lies he would offer as responses.

"So, what have you been up to?"

Umm, after being dismissed from Harvard, I have been

working as a clerk at this rare and used bookstore where I sell books to Harvard students and professors, including Dr. Mendelbaum, the churlish, bow-tie-wearing professor, oblivious to his own self-parodying fastidiousness, famous for his series of papers documenting the lovers of Lord Byron's lovers. He once served on my examination committee, who, finding my appreciation of Jane Austen wholly lacking, dismissed me. Who I must now smile at, sliding the leather-bound copy of *Sickness Unto Death*, 1849 first edition, across the wooden counter, cluttered with flyers for free public lectures and readings and making small talk as I swiped the Visa Titanium, praying for a fast connection.

"So, Stephen, you look well," said Mendelbaum, the bastard, feigning cordiality, Stephen could just tell.

"Thanks. Been reading much?" Stephen asked.

"A great deal, yes. I've got a paper I'll be presenting next month . . . well . . . I'm sure you're not interested in all that."

"No, I'm always trying to stay on top of life in the academy."

"Really? I would have thought . . ."

"That I'd have moved back to Detroit with my tail between my legs?"

"No, just the opposite actually. I would have thought that you would have applied to UNC, or Illinois-Chicago, like we'd spoken about. I'm certain that they would have taken you—a mind like yours."

Stephen steamed, *A small, pathetic mind like mine, barely able to comprehend the complexities of James Thurber, let alone James Joyce.*

"Really, Stephen, I think you could still have a go at it. I would be glad to help in anyway I could."

"Thanks, Professor. I'm pretty happy right now, things are going really well for me. I'm thinking about going into acting . . . I used to act a bit, you know."

"I remember your mentioning that. Well, good for you then. I guess that's that. Keep in touch though, will you, Stephen? I do miss seeing you."

Stephen wondered where all this concern and benevolence came from. Was it the 10 percent discount I gave him? Stephen refused to let himself be sucked into the professor's machinations. He could still feel the words those three months ago when he conferred with the committee following the oral examinations. Their words pummeled his midsection so that the wind was forced from his belly, followed by the tears, stinging, scalding his flesh, and the shame at the tears. He resolved to never cry again. The faint, damning praise echoed in his head for nights and weeks thereafter. "You've got a fine mind, Stephen, just not a Harvard mind." The smug emphasis on the word "Harvard," followed by just the slightest pause before the word "mind." Slight, but just long enough for the last syllable to rattle about the room a bit, almost visible to Stephen's eye so that he must fight the physical sensation to lurch after it, grasping at it, like a small boy after an eloping parakeet. Then the word "mind," repeated for emphasis, and the door slamming shut on his future as a brilliant scholar. There he stood, emasculated, the red-haired son of an Irish printer man, alone, a long way from Detroit.

This last bit of keyboarding wizardry was offered by my two-year-old daughter, who grabbed me by my hand and said, "Get up, Daddy." I was touched by her tender gesture, thinking she wanted me to play, and feeling guilty for writing this stupid book instead of eating bagels and watching *Blues Clues* with her and my wife, I complied. She had no intentions of playing with me; she climbed into my chair and began pounding on the keyboard and said "I did it." I chose to keep this in here so I can provide additional ammunition to the snide and lazy critics who can now say "The best part of Mr. Michael's new novel is the part written by his two-year-old daughter." And at least, David Michael's two-year-old has an excuse for writing such crap—she's only been speaking a few months—what's his excuse? Or "I found myself wondering if Mr. David Michaels had spent more time playing with his daughter instead of writing this book, perhaps the world would be a better place." Or for the especially mean critics—"The apple surely does not fall far from the tree, as evidenced by the incoherent ramblings of novelist David Michaels, and the haphazard keyboarding of his two-year-old daughter."

For those of you desiring resolution, David and Liz did not see Stephen on that trip to Boston.

Confessions

"Making movies is just like anything else, I suppose"—Liz.

"We had the script, we had the crew, we had the marketing plan. It was supposed to be one of those hyper-indyfreak things. Groundbreaking or some such silliness. You know, one of those made on a credit card, black-and-white Sundance things. Grainy and hand-held cameras. Lots of cursing and loud music. Hyper real. Super real. Really freaking real. Like every nightmare you ever had just thrown right up there on the screen and you're just ripped out of your head and you may as well be naked, for all you care."—Richard.

"It started off all beautiful and thrown together in a mix of friendship and love, and just an incredible lust, borne out of sadness as we race toward the infinite. It started out with death and it ended in death. Not to be all gloomy and bleak and morbid about things. Why minimize it? Each one of us lost something in this thing, and I'm not sure we gained something better in the final analysis. That's the thing that they don't tell you on those celebfreak interview shows, in the glossies or the blue neon enemas. That's the big secret. That's the thing—the world is full of folks just pimping their way through without telling it. That's the thing."—Stephen.

"Who knows, maybe in the end, we weren't ready. Ready for the real. Ready for the blood and the pus and the gut-wrench. Exhume. Maybe we weren't ready to 'tell the truth that is a lie,' or some such pithy crap. Maybe we weren't pithy enough. Thin and black-leathered enough."—Richard.

"I thought myself that making this movie would bring us all closer. Stephen, the superstar. Richard, the cyberpoet. Elizabeth, the singer of pureness—neither Madonna nor whore but pure.

Me—David, the quiet one. You've seen us before a zillion times. We're in every movie, every television show, and every really bad novel. You know who we are. We are post-nuclear anti-Jungian archetypes, not ancient and eternal but created for a discrete segment of time, namely the time it takes you to read this book (two-four hours max). Then we will be deleted from your memory like some Czechoslovakian communist party boss who fell out of favor in 1948, or 1959, or 1967. Do not make an effort to document our existence in underground, photocopied fanzines or websites. Do not scrawl our names with black spray paint on the overpasses along I-94."—David.

"We are you."—Liz.

Don't Go Back to Westville

It is odd to think that a high school named for William Carlos Williams would be located in suburban Detroit, especially in one as bland and annoying as Westville. But that is where the four of us spent our formative years. Not that many of the schools with almost 2,000 students had any idea who the Bard of Paterson was. Those of us who had AP English read *The Red Wheel Barrow* and that one about the cold plums, but that was about it. It could have been named Hubert Humphrey High School and meant just as little to the student body. I wish there were something quaint and curious I could impress you with about Westville. Mr. T did not live here. There are no unusual religious cults or nuclear reactors. There are no bizarre quadruple homicides several days before Christmas, well, just one, but it is statistically insignificant.

Westville was built as a bedroom community, a mere three miles from Detroit's western borders, about fourteen miles via Francis Turner's highways to the corner of Washington Boulevard and Michigan, in the mid-1950s, a real nice place to live. About 100,000 of the nicest lower middle-class white folk living in 1,000-foot, three-bedroom brick ranches. (I did not realize I was lower middle class until I went to college and met my roommate, who was from the "middle class"—his term—suburb in Westchester County, New York, tan and fit from his recent safari to Kenya. We went to Mammoth Caves that summer and slept in a tent. Three miles, but that could be three miles across the Empty Quarter, or on top of Mt. Everest, or across the River Styx, for the amount of black-and-white intermingling that went on. Our high school had two black students, that is what we called them then. I was not hip to the term "African-American" until my wonderful eye-opening experience at that great bastion of liberalism, the University of Michigan in Ann Arbor. The black students were from a group home for "troubled youth." They may have been troubled, but they were revered by many of the white kids at my school as gods. Rap was breaking out big and Fab Five jerseys could have been the official school uniform.

I was kicked out of U of M, but still hanging around when the Fab Five won the national championship, or should I say, won, with an asterisk. Richard and I were sitting around his apartment on Ann Street, playing video games when we heard a bunch of people yelling and car horns honking. We decided to go outside and were swept away with the rising tide of euphoric basketball fans that led us to South University. It was a surreal scene. I know, I know. You sort of cringe whenever you read that phrase "surreal scene." It's usually not very surreal at all, just a bit silly, or annoying, or different. But as Richard had recently finished a course in Art History, he guaranteed that we had indeed experienced a surreal experience. There were thousands of people standing on the street in the cold, but it was oddly quiet. People were standing around looking at each other and making normal, quiet conversation. "It sure is great our team won." "Boy, that sure was some basketball game." That sort of thing. Every now and then, someone would scream "WE WONNN!" and the crows would whoop for a moment or two and drivers would politely honk their horns a few times. I can't quite figure out why we were so subdued, or for that matter, why we even bothered to walk the six blocks in the cold. It's not like "we" won the game, or that "we" did anything except subsidize their basketball experience with our parents' tuition money. We, Richard and I, hadn't even remembered the game was on. I suspect those naked fellows hanging from the traffic signal in front of Charley's had a different take on the evening entirely. In retrospect, they did seem to be enjoying themselves in a way that I never have been able to.

I suppose that is the fundamental problem I have with society. I don't get it. I mean, much of it, that is, those things that are done for enjoyment, amusement, or even leisure, I generally find strange or irritating. I wish I could be like those writers and artists who also appreciated professional competition. Like Spike Lee and Woody Allen loving the Knicks, or George Will adoring baseball. I have turned exceedingly dull as I have grown older. No wonder I do not have any friends. Still, you have to be fair; you have to admit that there is much to find amusing about fan behavior. Grown men in jerseys, for example. People standing around a fire in a metal barrel in a gravel-paved, broken-bottle-strewn, barbed-wire-fenced parking lot near a burned-out brick movie theater with gang graffiti scrawled on it at 10:30 A.M. on a Sunday morning, eating chips and hot dogs they are grilling themselves, with a half-gallon bottle of Jim Beam, opened and **half finished**, standing and openly urinating as parents with young boys walk past, eagerly heading to watch the Lions. Maybe, that's the part that I don't get. Perhaps, these folks were recently reawakened from a comatose state and they don't realize the Lions have not won a game in, like, eight or nine years. These are the same people who would probably laugh when I tell them about our plans for the documentary about James Joyce. They'd be all like, "James Joyce, who the hell cares about that guy? He should have stopped with 'Dubliners.' Anything after that was just a rehashing of his earlier themes, done with much more hot air than any effort to illuminate." Or something like that. Or they might demonstrate their thuggish nationalism and posit, "There are plenty of great American writers to do a documentary about, why not someone like George Oppen? Or even better, someone who is still living and has something to say? What about Wendy Lesser, for God's sake?"

Richard and Stephen met in second grade at Bohr Academy, a magnet school in our district for nascent genii. There was no formal curriculum or assessments. To hear them tell it, the days were spent eating glue or designing contraptions to improve the waste elimination process of felines. Apparently, Stephen really hated cleaning his cat's litter box. Lizzie met them in seventh grade, when her family moved here from Grand Rapids, her father having been kicked out of the Calvinist Church for betting on college basketball games. I met them in the tenth grade, in Ms. Belonski's accelerated English class. I was eating my peanut butter and jelly sandwich and side order of tater tots at a table alone and overheard them talking about a "plus four long sword" and had to interject that an elf would never use such a weapon. We became fast friends. I must admit, I felt like an outsider with the three of them a lot then, and still do, even though I am married to Lizzie. Sometimes when they get together, they communicate on some sort of sublingual level, phrases and grunts passing for sentences, and bits of Gilbert and Sullivan lyrics as the punchline to way too many jokes. I know it is time to drag Lizzie by the collar and head to bed when they start breaking into "Johnny One Note" from "Babes in Arms," as it is only a matter of time before they start breaking out the Sondheim, and as I am one of those people who don't appreciate artists until they're dead . . .

Yes, they do sound like the kind of people you would want to despise, and I often do. But not always, and not nearly as much for those traits as for others that I will tell you about, and to be fair, not as much as I want to despise the people who stole the reindeer off my front lawn or threw snow balls at me while I was out running, or those wearing the Detroit Lions jersey who urinated openly in the parking lot as my family drove to church on Sunday morning. And certainly not as much as I despise myself at least ten times a day, mostly for being so lazy and wasting my time, despising everybody else.

A False Passing

No one else was in the house when Stephen's dad passed away. Mother was at work and his sister, Jinny, was at the movies watching one of the *Naked Gun* movies with her boyfriend. She was seventeen, almost eighteen at the time, and had twice won state competitions in Irish dance. Mother, Fiona, was a cashier at the local supermarket, Jack's IGA, for those of you keeping score at home. Very lower middle class, see? Brick ranch house, no basement, and one-car garage, built in the 1950's for cagey GI's. Stephen went to the grocery store, but not the one his mother worked at. He wasn't in the mood. You know, all the small talk with the baggers and cashiers, and the limp handshake and tit jokes from the assistant manager, "Karl with a K, not a C, see?" whom Stephen went to William Carlos Williams High School with. Stephen was in no mood for the meager jokes about Stephen's life in the "Big City" (Chicago) as a "Big Superstar" (struggling actor). Jokes of the "I'll bet you're too big to buy your own pork rinds these days." All kinds of, "Hey, we'll see you next year at the big ten-year reunion," and "Where the hell were you at the five-year reunion? Shooting a big-time movie, I'll bet, hey, superstar?" His mother commented on how smart he is and how he should be a lawyer and how his younger sister won a scholarship to Michigan. "Tuition and room and board." Stephen wasn't in the mood, and who could blame him, with his dad dying of cancer and everybody keenly aware that those may be more than just thunderclouds on the horizon? They could be clouds of fire or clouds of death. That's what they could be according to the cashier/astrologers. Stephen, being much more rational, realized that all living things die, it's like the circle of life in that cool Disney movie. He also realized that eventually, individuals with inoperable cancer die, regardless of the alignment of stars or clouds, even if one of these people were your father, whom you believed from a young age would live forever.

The New Face of Hemorrhoids

It should be noted that several months prior, Stephen began a daily regimen of coffee enemas—you can never be too sure, especially as that mysterious spot of blood developed in his stool—hemorrhoids, thank god. Can you believe that was one of the questions they asked him at the audition for the hemorrhoid commercial? It wasn't the agent; it was some pink-faced, jowly man, Fred Tomlinson, who worked for the drug company that made this new anti-hemorrhoid cream.

"The only reason I ask is that we believe in our product, and we want everybody involved in this project to be as committed as we are. We think this product will bring major relief to millions of Americans, hopefully to millions of Canucks, too—they've got a lot of hemorrhoids over there too. Did you know that Americans lead the world in hemorrhoid sufferers? I'll bet you did not know that—not many people do. Do you know why? It's not what you think—it's not because we sit all day at our jobs. I mean, that's part of it—Americans sit an awful lot. Two reasons—Americans produce more excrement per person than the entire EU combined—'cause we eat so much—we got to get rid of it somehow, don't we? You betcha we do. Number two reason—we read on the can. The average American spends seven to nine minutes per excretion episode, the average person in Denmark—ninety seconds! Isn't that incredible? Did you know that more Americans suffer from hemorrhoids than any other disease? And don't you think for a second that hemorrhoids are not a disease. Anyone who knows will tell you it is. Granted, it's not as bad as cancer or what have you, but it is a major, major problem. Did you know that over hemorrhoid sufferers lose an average of eleven days of work per year due to hemorrhoid-related illness? I'll bet you did not know that . . . So you see, we think this is a very, very serious issue for our company, and for Americans all over the world. We aren't looking for just an actor; we are looking for a hero. Someone who can put a human face on hemorrhoids."

"I see," Stephen said. "I would like to be that person. As a recent hemorrhoid sufferer, I know firsthand the pain, the turmoil, and let's be honest, the embarrassment of being a hemorrhoid sufferer. But I am not ashamed to say it. I have hemorrhoids! Mr. Tomlinson, I want to represent your company, I want to make a difference. I want to be the new face of hemorrhoids!"

Stephen made more being the "new face of hemorrhoids" in 110 hours of work, over several commercials, than I did in three years as a full-time social worker (with a master's degree), and about five thousand times higher than any compensation for my writing three issues of the *New Detroit Review* at six bucks each. Not that I'm resentful or anything. I guess the cost of living in Chicago or Los Angeles is a bit higher than here in the Hometown of Henry Ford (it's on the official city letter head—I swear to god.) Besides, he burned it all in airfare, flying back and forth to visit his dad, God bless him.

A Sort of Homecoming

Stephen returned from the grocery store and pulled the rented Buick Century, silver, four-door, into the driveway of the three-bedroom, brown, brick ranch house and cut out the lights and the radio. It was some bland modern rock hit (registered trademark). He pulled out two brown bags of groceries, always chosen over plastic, and walked to the front door. Whole wheat bread, apples, orange juice, yogurt, tofu, lean turkey breast, diet cola, Boston Leaf lettuce, red-raspberry vinaigrette salad dressing, Dijon mustard, a Riesling—the essentials for a few days at home. The pork chops and mashed potatoes, or green bean casserole—Fiona's famous, went straight to his gut and jowl. He set one of the bags down, fumbled with the keys and finally opened the door. He walked in the silence of the house to the kitchen and set the bags on the counter, and then flicked on the lights. He looked at the digital clock on the stove—9:30 P.M. He checked the messages—none. He then put away the groceries—apples, cereal, milk, orange juice, barbecue, potato chips, and several cans of baked beans.

He sat at the table and poured himself a bowl of cereal and milk. He commented to himself on how bad the cereal box designs are now compared to when he was a kid. @ They always have some tie-in to the latest animated kids' movie that just looks retarded. Who are the "Space Knights" or "Ned Nebularino?" Are these people on crack or what? He ate the cereal, rinsed out the bowl and set it in the sink, reminding himself to put it in the dishwasher later, after a trip to the lavatory.

He knew he should check on his dad, who had just returned from the St. Margaret's two days ago because of not eating anything. He knew he should check and see his dad, just as he had dozens of times before, but he did not want to. He looked at the clock: 9:41.

A Parenthetical Observation

@This section was written after I had read Hemingway's Nick Adams stories again prior to rewrites.

A Return to the Scene

He walked back to the sink and had a glass of water. His mother worked until 10:00 P.M., and she wouldn't actually get home until 10:20 P.M. or so. If he waited long enough, she would be the one that would have to check on Dad, not him, not Stephen, the eldest son, the actor, first family college graduate, the first US citizen, the liar. He had done this death scene before, explored the emotions involved, gotten in touch with several of them, created a space where he could simply be. And every time, he hated going to that place, even as he was telling himself that he was Strong Stephen, that he was Spiritual Stephen, and every time, he felt a stab of guilt for making it all about him, and not the dying or dead father in the next room.

9:53 P.M. Only thirty minutes until Mom comes home. The first words out of her mouth will be, "Have you checked on

Dad?" Not even a "hello" or "Good to see you," or even "Did you get the goddamn groceries?" It won't even be "How's your father feeling tonight?" It'll be "Have you checked on your father?" She can play the dutiful wife and the guilt-inducing mother in one clever bit of rhetoric.

Bitch. I shouldn't give her the pleasure. Still, I could lie about it, I am an actor, after all. I could not go check on Dad but say I did. I'll say, "Of course, of course, I checked on him." I'm very talented and majored in theater at university; she'll never know the difference. If she checks on him and he's dead, then I'll be shocked and say, "He must have recently expired." If he's alive, then, I'll of course be relieved, and no one will be the worse for it. What if she asks Colin Darden, the father of our hero, Stephen Darden, whether Stephen had adequately attended to his needs, and the father replied that he had heard some rustling in the kitchen, possibly the sound of some cereal being consumed? Therefore, he assumed Stephen was home, but had not actually seen his son since his son had returned home earlier that evening. What if this was to occur? And wouldn't it be just like her to ask such a question, to try to catch Stephen in one of his lies? Even as a child, the boy lied, she told Eleanor and Miriam at the grocery store. Why, when he was seven years he even convinced the doctor at St. Martha's Emergency that he had some burning sensation in his peeper, and was seeing double—all to get out of taking a spelling test that he didn't study for! What a riot that boy was. His father laughed a bit too, until he saw that hospital bill! Didn't stop the boy from lying, though, even following the intimate discussion with the belt leather! Always knew he'd be a great actor, which was a lie, of course, but it was better for her than admitting to her friends that not only had her son been dismissed from a Harvard doctoral program—some sort of literature or another, and from the University of Chicago, where he was briefly employed as a website developer, but that he was an essentially unemployed actor who was famous for his hemorrhoid commercials.

The phone rang. He lunged for it, clicking it on as he spun for the remote control, ending on his tiptoes. "Hello," he said with perhaps a bit too much enthusiasm.

It was me on the other line. "Hey what's up . . . you're in town?"

"Yeah, just got in a few hours ago. Dad's not doing well."

"Sorry, is there anything I can do?"

"No, I guess his lungs keep filling up with fluid, and the cancer has pretty much spread all through his body. It's in his bones now . . ."

He was thinking, "So it's just a matter of time." I was thinking that too. Looking back, I realized it's always a matter of time. But as someone who was a neophyte in the death realm, I only thought in clichés and pathetic greeting-card jingoism. "Hey, you've got to celebrate each moment." Or "Hey, it's only in suffering that we get to experience true love." My favorite, "Suffering is the pathway to enlightenment." I can't tell you how many cards at the Hallmark store have that one, usually with a picture of a puppy dog at the guillotine from the great Canine Tribunal of the fourteenth century.

Realtime Alert: As I type this into my computer at 8:46 P.M. on Saturday, July 6, 2002, my next-door neighbor, DA Peckerhead (Dumb Ass) is revving his piece-of-shit, mid-1980s black Monte Carlo for four minutes. A person of a haughty disposition may be sitting in the comfort of a leather recliner, drinking a glass of 1998 Rosalind Estates Cabernet and saying four minutes is a mere trifle. Some people who enjoy loud noises and banging metal as the Nazareth song "Son of a Bitch" pounds from the open garage and the smell of car exhaust billows through their bedroom window may consider me fortunate. I am neither one of those types of people. If you were to set your super-cool triathlon watch alarm for four minutes, and then either sit completely still without moving a single muscle (your heart doesn't count, I'm not expecting you to stop your heart for four minutes, unless you're so inclined), or you can bang your head against a cinderblock wall for four minutes. Either way, you will begin to understand what the four minutes of daily car-revving experience is for us. It is now 8:54 P.M. and the bedroom still smells like auto exhaust, as does the dining room. For some reason, he backs the muffler-less wonder out of his garage and has the rear of the car parked right outside of this bedroom window, a distance of approximately eight feet. As bad as the experience is for me, it is far worse for my wife, Mrs. David Michaels, as she had spent the preceding fifty-two minutes trying to put our daughter, the Daughter of Mr. and Mrs. David Michaels (I am protecting her identity so her peers at the day care do not hound her for my autograph and requests to sing at their birthday parties all the time), to sleep. An experience that has grown into a challenge of almost biblical proportions. Think Moses versus the Egyptian Army. Needless to say, the combination screeching tires and misgauged spark plugs on a revving V8 engine sans muffler, with Nazareth cranked to ensure the effect of its subtle melodic inventions would not be lost to those of us within three blocks, was enough to wake up our daughter—aged two. I hear the shrill scream over the baby monitor now, "No don't let the car monster get me," as my wife rushes upstairs, swearing at Mr. Peckerhead and our ineffectual city government, who has lent no support in our efforts to oust our good neighbor. I will provide updates as they occur so as to keep you apprised of this ongoing crisis.

Back to The Show

As I was saying, I didn't know what the hell to say to Stephen and he didn't know what to say to me, but he was sure glad to hear from me, so he didn't want to let me go that easily.

"Hey, did you hear the new *Yo La Tengo* disc?"

"No, not yet. I heard it's great, do you like it?"

"Oh yeah, it's great. It's a bit more mellow than their last, but, it's still amazing. Beautiful harmonies."

"Sounds good. Hey, what did your dad say about the debates?"

"What could he say, Clinton was incredible. The man looks so smooth, so just, just like on the money. He looks so ridiculously smart, especially next to those other chicken heads."

"Yeah, but how can a guy that smart like Kenny G? I mean, what does that tell you? Well, what do you want from a guy from Arkansas?"

"Don't you live in the Motor City, the hometown of burning bubba and Ted Nugent?"

"Mr. Nugent is simply misunderstood. It's all an act, sort of like Howard Stern or Rush Limbaugh. Underneath the bluster is a real keen intellect and sophisticated sensibility. I find their satires of post-Reagan American consumerism fiercely original."

We both laughed.

"So, any word from Richard?" I asked.

"Not too much. I got an email from him the other day. He'll be in town for Christmas. I guess his sister is getting married. Too bad."

"What about the script?"

"I haven't done anything on it, and I doubt Richard has. What about you guys?"

"Yeah, I've been doing some stuff. I've got some notes. Did you know Joyce was a huge fan of cinema?"

"Really? No, I didn't, that really surprises me. I mean, with him being so blind and all. And what the hell, movies existed back then? 'Birth of a Nation' or some Shirley Temple thing?"

"Well, I don't know if he really liked the movies, but it would be a hell of a thing if he did. I just read Kafka liked movies though, so why the hell wouldn't Joyce?"

"No one will ever know, anyway. If they see it on the silver screen, they'll believe it."

"Especially if we have some guy with glasses and a beard saying it."

"Someone with a slight eastern European accent. Harsh syllables and all that."

"It'll be beautiful."

"I have a feeling people will weep. They will weep openly when they see this. It will be beautiful."

"Without question, it will be beautiful."

*This last sequence brought to you by the Save David Mamet Foundation, who kindly provided a grant to finish this novel.

10:19. The rattling oil pan of his mother's 1989 Cavalier as it crawled into the driveway. Damn, I got to get in there and check on Dad. He's okay, he's okay, he's okay. Our father who art in heaven . . . goddamn, what is the next line? I can't believe I forgot the "Our Father," he chuckled to himself. The car door slammed and mother opened the trunk to grab a bag of groceries. She would be in the house in less than ten seconds. Fifteen tops.

He took a deep breath and walked across the hallway to his dad's room. Slowly, he opened the door and stood in the doorway with his eyes closed for a moment. He felt somewhat lightheaded but he opened his eyes.

His father lay askew from the torso onto the bedcovers. His head faced away from the doorway. Stephen's heart jumped as he walked over to the side of the bed, astonished at his father's gaunt face . . . He stood for a moment and the memory of his father's round and ruddy face smiling above him, reading him *Alice in Wonderland*, stinking of whiskey and cigarettes, rushed over him, filling him with emotion. There was a sound like sandpaper scraping gently on pine that emanated from his father's throat—a faint sign of life. Stephen bent over and picked up a hardcover copy of *Ulysses,* brown, Modern Library, with the dust jacket removed, which fell open on the green carpet. He stood in the yellow lamplight, staring and sobbing.

Stephen wiped his eyes, placed the book on the Furio nightstand, turned off the lamp, and stood for a moment longer in the doorway. He thought he should return and place the bed sheets back across his father's outstretched body. I mustn't wake him. He needs his rest. "I love you, Da," words which fell into the thick mud of deathwatch and sloughed through it before landing gently on his father's ashen cheek. His father stirred slightly as Stephen turned and walked to the kitchen where his mother was waiting.

She turned from the stove, where she was placing the blue kettle on to boil water for tea, and stared straight at him as he entered. Her oval, ruddy face was drawn and tired, and her hair was mostly gray, shocking him, a strand falling across her hazel eyes. In her blue-and-red polyester cashier's outfit, she looked plump, but not stately.

"Jesus, Stephen, it's good to see you. You're looking good, son. Come and give your mother a hug." Her lilting Irish voice was even more musical then he remembered, as he'd of late been immersed in the thick staccato of the city of big shoulders. In contrast, hers was thick, amber, honey that he could taste simply by sticking out his tongue and licking the words out of the air.

He said, "How's it going, Mom?" or "Good to see you, Mom," or some other such pleasantry. It really didn't matter to them, or to me, what he said. He was a full head taller than her, so he stooped to wrap his arms around her thick waist, and he squeezed her. She felt as permanent as an oak tree, immovable even in the face of it all. She smelled of sweat and perfume and cigarettes, but he soaked it in like it was the salty air blowing off the coast of the Isle of Skye. She patted his shoulders and sniffled, fighting a flood of tears poised at the ducts, primed, ready to burst forth and shower down upon them both. Even though she knew it would be good for both of them to bathe in that salty river, become borne anew, baptized, she held back with all her might. Her knees trembled at the strain. Now is not the time for tears, she thought, and squeezed him so tightly he thought his back would snap. He did not care. His only thought was crawling inside her, through her vagina, curling into a tiny fetus and going to sleep. Home again.

Colin Darden would expire the next night at 9:30 P.M.

Sneak Preview

The four are silent.

The camera pulls from the screen to the three seated on folding chairs, watching the film. A white, stucco-walled room, dark, save for the gyre of light from the projector onto the screen. The dusty vertical blinds clack softly with the intermittent breeze. Annoyingly warm, not refreshing.

Stephen stood with his hands in his jeans pockets, watching himself on the silver screen, grainy, colors washed, and mouthing along silently to himself the words coming from the cassette recorder in a very small voice.

Stephen

Slowly: Tears. This is not the time for tears. Tears have dried up now. Tears have gone away. Now, we must smile. We must be happy in our hearts and we must smile, as he is surely smiling at us. Without pain. Without fear. Smiling down at us. The snow, falling faintly through the universe and across the living and the dead. He memorized these words, ever so wrongly but ever so beautifully, and dreamt them. In his sleep. In his peacefulness. In his quietness. He dreamt them. Himself floating among the snowflakes. Himself floating across the embalmed fields of Ireland. Home again.

The film circles out and the four stare at the white screen.

Moments pass.

Stephen turns off the projector and smiles. Pass, pass more moments, more. Stephen connects his eyes to mine. I had been there before the film. I do not know what to say. How could you do this? I hear myself say. Steal your own words from your own other self and steal them. The death.

Stephen smiles.

I say aloud—Powerful.

He knows this, of course. Of course he does. At the least, it is that.

But why no tears—the Irishness?
He asks, "You don't think its too sentimental?"
Sentimental.
Of senses.
Of sensuality.
What is the proper decorum for offering constructive feedback to your best friend who had re-enacted the eulogy he spoke at his father's funeral for a film you are making about James Joyce's eyes? I smile my dopey smile and wait five seconds. Nothing clever or suitably dissembling came to mind, so I simply lied.

"It was pitch perfect. I wouldn't change a thing."

There we—you were. Sitting four in the living room. Stephen, the zero-smiling, red-hair-faced. From the heart. Then Richard, the Anglican, the ears and all. Me and Liz. Blind to what was happening, what they were saying, all those pretty words painted in pretty colors. We four in the summer heat, the air thick with itself. Thick with the burdens of its memory of itself. Thick indeed with the water. Unholy, but necessary indeed. Indeed.

Stephen rises from the brown wicker chair. Crosses, bare feet fall on the brown carpet.

The Film Begins Here

A tight shot of Stephen's face. Slender cheeks, pale and red. Health/sick Irish boy/man. The click, click, the click, click. The 16-mm projector we stole from the film co-op. The noses and the ears. I forgot the others. It is the wind which spews? Black venom. Blake's ve non. But does the wind sense? Of sense? Of sensuality? It is the sins' black dent on black feet, but dost sin repent? Man, O—the fallibility of words linked to thoughts, not to senses, to sentence, to sentiments, lines of ink on a page, electrons on a screen, which exist despite.

Man, O'Mann.
Man, O' Rourke.
Kosciusko.

General George Washingpatton.
Your puppy died.
Your puppy died in your arms.

You hold a photograph of you at age eight, holding your puppy. Brand-new puppy, and you are holding it. A beagle. Brown and black fur and moist nose and bright, shiny eyes stare directly at the camera. Your father has a knife at the throat of your puppy. Is it a butcher's knife or a butter knife? Your father has a steak knife in his left hand and there is blood. You recall it is Thursday and there is always blood. You mustn't cry though, or it will be worse for everyone. Was it my mother who said that? Was it my father? And the father drops the beagle to the floor and the beagle runs over to you and begins licking your face, licking the tears, the buckets of salty tears pouring from your eyes that were anguish and now euphoria, and the dog is licking the tears. You touch his soft fur, and you hug him close to you and feel his hot breath and his wet tongue tickling on your face and you laugh your red freckles off.

"Next time he shits in the house, its for real," your father says as he walks to the sink to run his hand under cold water to stop the blood from flowing from the place where he cut himself with the steak knife.

Richard told me that story about his dad and the puppy at Da Vinci's Italian Ristorante, the site of the wake. Good place for the wake of an Irishman, don't you think? Stephen's father would say anyplace there's whiskey is a good place for the wake of an Irishman. I never could tell if Richard was telling the truth or if it was one of his put-ons. He was always saying crazy stuff and most of the time, you would not believe him and he'd end up to be telling the truth, and then when you did believe him, he'd start laughing because he knew he had you. It was hard to spend a lot of time with Richard.

Yule-esses

The only one of us who actually read *Ulysses* prior to making the movie was Stephen. He studied it as an undergrad at Waterloo

College, sitting under the poster of U2 (*War* era) and Jimi Hendrix, crouching over his burning guitar—wasn't that taken at the Isle of Wight Festival in England? which thankfully covered the gray cinderblock walls. I had read only *Araby*, which we read in AP English, and *Portrait of an Artist*. I didn't get much of either one at the time I read them. I kind of think Joyce is like that for the modern reader. He focuses too much on words and language and such—the curse of many an otherwise fine writer. I guess maybe that's why I only got a "3" on my AP exams. Still, if you aren't thinking film rights, then you really shouldn't call yourself a writer.

It was Christmas time and Stephen was home for the Christmas holiday, the first one as an adult, a college freshman, and a U.S. citizen, which had ominous implications for a true modern Yuletide, much more *Santaland Diaries* or *The Great Santa* than *A Boy's Christmas in Wales*, despite the Darden family's authentic IRISH HERITAGE.

I hope you appreciate my use of the word "holiday" in the preceding paragraph. After a long deliberation, including reviewing Barzun's *Simple and Direct*, several Safire columns, a Buckley essay, a *Doonesbury* strip, and consulting my wife and daughter, my sixth-grade teacher, Miss Nicely (the name chosen because it is a synonymous pseudonym for her real name, which my sixth-grade best friend, Steve Turner's mom, said reminded her of a character in some 1930s gangster movie), the word "holiday" was chosen over the more commonly used Midwestern term of "vacation." We also conducted several focus groups and they preferred the word "holiday" to the word "vacation." Apparently, there is a classic documentary film series profiling an American family struggling to retain their individual and collective identities and familial traditions in the face of mass-marketed consumer culture having the word "vacation" in the title, which would be very confusing to the reader of this book and the subsequent movie. Also, as I understand it, "holiday" is the preferred term in the Emerald Isle, indeed in all of the United Kingdom of Great Britain and Northern Ireland, and did I mention that Stephen and family were all IRISH? Did I mention that James Joyce, the author, who plays a prominent part in the imagery of our movie, was also IRISH? Did I mention that unlike Manhattan in the nineteenth century, IRISH tests very well in most urban markets, including San Jose, California, Chicagoland, and even Boston, Massachusetts? Even many simple folk who live in places like Toledo, Ohio, Grand Rapids, Michigan, and Chapel Hill, North Carolina, have strong "positive" feelings (at least a 4 on a 5-point likert scale). If I can get 1 percent of the people who drink green beer on St. Patrick's Day to purchase a copy of this book (they don't even have to read it), then I will have enough money to pay off my student loans and afford a new minivan, so that maybe we can take a camping trip to Nova Scotia, and I will not have to teach summer school! If I were to get the number of people who pay money to see the Detroit Lions lose at home on ANY GIVEN SUNDAY (thanks for the donation, Al) to purchase a copy of this book, my wife could probably go down to part time and spend more time with our wonderful children. I, being the hard-driven, type A personality that I am, would never consider an extended vacation, solely designed to count my cash, even if the number of people who watched the lowest-rated television show on a major network on Wednesday during prime time were to buy my book. I am so dedicated, in fact, that I am not enjoying this brief holiday/vacation from my day job to slave away at this novel, not in the hopes of actually seeing a penny of profit, but because I love words and simply want to share this joy with as many people as I can, and to prove that maybe, even though I was kicked out of a major university and made over 60 percent less per year in the 1990s as a social worker than a first-year electrical engineer at one of the Big Three, and who has only three minuscule publication credits to his CV, and whose band never made more than $200 bucks on a gig in over five years, a CD, and several cool 7" singles, that I am not a complete and utter failure who cannot complete anything. So, if using the goddamn word "holiday" is going to sell a few more books, then join the line and sue me.

Won't you all feel ashamed and petty when you realize that I actually come from a family that is both a political dynasty and obscenely wealthy (not unlike the Kennedys, who, if I'm not mistaken, are also IRISH), and am writing this book on a lark.

Stephen walked into his parents' home on Crabapple Lane on December 21, and instantly became repulsed. The smell of cigarette smoke mixed with pot roast in a most unsavory manner. His entrance was masked by the sound of Pat and Vanna at a volume slightly lower than required to actually shatter the glass windows, which were vibrating in their panes when the commercials came on. His father was on the brown corduroy recliner, legs up, the purple-and-maroon shawl draped casually across his legs so only his gray slippers were visible. His head was angled back so his mouth pointed upward towards the ceiling, agape, almost as if a reservoir for the cobwebs clinging to the corner of the curtain rod, nearly above him. The mucus and spit rattled in the back of his throat like Velcro ripping apart, the myriad clasps never completely releasing their grip. His face was lugubrious—pasty, gray and sunken in the blue waves of the television. There were no lights on in the house. His dad looked so sick and so old that had he not heard the noises emanating from his throat, he would have thought his father was dead. Fuck it. Why the detachment? Why the conditional tenses and the obsessive recounting of details? Why the defenses? Of course, this is what we all do when looking into the abyss—assume a posture that makes us see the beautiful flowers, and not the decapitated babies. Underneath the thick walls of reason and rationalization, almost completely unaware of him, Stephen screamed at the sight of his dead father.

His mother called out from the kitchen, "Stephen? Come on in, love, give your mum a kiss."

He walked into the kitchen and saw his mother setting out a frozen dinner of pot roast, mashed potatoes and peas. She didn't look any different. Her brown hair was cut short, naturally ungray, belying her sixty-three years on this planet. He stooped over and gave her a hug on her thick waist and strong embrace, stopping for a moment the headache that had been building up.

"What's up with Dad? He sick or something?"

"No, dear, what makes you say that?"

"Well, he looks like shit, for one thing. He's passed out in front of *Wheel of Fortune*, not swearing at the stupid contestants, and it sounds like he's got sandpaper in his lungs."

"Oh, he's probably just tired," she said as she turned to the stove to pick up the teakettle with a hot pad, only to set it immediately down again."

"Mom, what's wrong?" Stephen said.

"Did you have a good train ride in?"

"I didn't take the train this time, remember? I flew in."

"That's right. Jesus, I'd forget my own head if it wasn't attached sometimes. I'll bet it was nice not to have to sit with all those 'rednecks and retards' on the train, as you like to call them. Have a seat, Stephen, your dinner is ready. You like pot roast, don't you?"

"Mom, I've been a vegetarian for over a year know. Remember last Christmas, we had that big conversation after Dad almost threatened to kick my 'communist ass' out of the house?"

"Well, yes, now that you say it, I guess I do remember that. Surely, you're hungry . . . a little pot roast never hurt anyone—its' good—just try it."

"Mom, I don't want pot roast. I never liked pot roast, always thought it tasted like shoe leather, and it's even worse when you lather it in nicotine."

"You're not going to get started on that this time, are you? Oh, Stephen, I really wish you wouldn't . . . We all know smoking is harmful. We all know it is the nectar of Hades, or however you used to call it. We know that Stephen, for God's sake. We know that. Please . . . for once, just . . . just don't talk about it . . ."

"Okay, Mom. He has cancer, doesn't he?"

"Oh God, Stephen, stop it. Cancer? You're always so dramatic. He has a chest cold or something—this miserable rainy weather. And he's spending too much goddamn time at the track, if you ask me. It'll be the death of him, I tell you."

"Has he been to the doctor's?"

"Of course not. You know your father doesn't need to go see those 'charlatans,' as he calls them, and to be fair to your father, he has seen some pretty dubious characters parading around like their next messiah in his day. Remember when I was sick back in 1977 and he kept telling the doctors, 'Take another look, there's something wrong with her, take another look,' and they kept giving him the royal brush-off, like he's some fucking immigrant just off the boat, like he's not an intelligent man? Stephen, how many American high school dropouts can quote you from *Macbeth*, I ask you? And if he did not keep begging and arguing, and really it wasn't until he found that Mary Flanagan, that nice, red-haired nurse whose family came from County Clare, you remember her, don't you, Stephen? She was such a smart girl, and beautiful. If it wasn't for your father tracking her down and getting her to talk to the doctors, I'd be dead. I swear to you I'd be dead."

"Mom, we've got to talk him into going to the doctor's. Can Jinny talk to him? He usually listens to her."

She looked into the teacup she had poured as she talked and swirled around the bag at the edge of the stainless steel spoon, and smiled, "I'm glad you're home, son. Tell me about your finals."

Stephen chose to drop the subject. His mother was through with it, for tonight, at least. A year ago, he would have badgered her and yelled and went into the living room and woken his father up and yelled at him too, and threatened to call EMS if his father didn't swear to God Almighty to go to the doctor the first thing in the morning. Although he desperately wanted to do this, to succumb to the anger and fear that was imbued in his blood cells, coursing through his heart and his brain, he didn't. The significance of this choice as an instance of growing maturity only became noteworthy in future reflection. For now, it felt good to be home, sitting in the kitchen, drinking tea and talking to his mom, as if he was playing out some happy memory.

Freshman Year—First Semester—Sorry, Folks, It's Legally Mandated that These Scenes be included if you're an author of a certain age (over thirty) and writing your first novel.

Stephens' roommate during his freshman year at Waterloo College was typical of the smart, rich, Caucasian, and suburban student who attended such private, four-year liberal arts schools in the Michigan hinterlands, chosen to ensure diversity so that all strains of liberalism are tolerated on campus. He had been on a safari with his family the previous summer. He interned at *Rolling Stone* first semester senior year in high school, and for a drunken East Coast senator that summer. Apparently, this senator has a thing for young boys with back freckles, which Stephen's roommate (who has not signed a release to let me use his name) indulged in many hours of back rubs at weekend "meetings" in a small coastal estate on the Atlantic, in a state that begins with either M or N, but which is definitely not North Carolina, or New Jersey, as the senators from those states and their attorneys have asked that I make perfectly clear. Apparently, the first 1,000 copies of this book, which I was required to "donate" to the law firms of one of these Good-Hearted, Brave, and Diligent Stewards of Democracy, made quite a bonfire at Senator *&^^#*&*#'s pig roast on %$#*$* Island.

The roommate, Enrico Gabriel Santiago (fictitious name), born to Elizabeth Taylor (fictitious but equally unintentionally absurd), daughter of the seatbelt-cover magnate, and Jasper Taylor, was considered conservative, in that neither parent actually had been sprayed at by a water cannon while attempting to organize workers at Waltermart in the late 1970s. Enrico was sitting barefoot on his bed, wearing jeans and a pink polo shirt, mouth engulfing a twelve-inch bong when Stephen walked in.

"Hey, how's it going?" Enrico asked.

Stephen observed that his roommate was notable for the lack of any noticeable Hispanic inflection in his speech and for the lack of alteration of voice patterns due to the herbal influence. Enrico had a clear, relaxed baritone which, if anything, seemed to have an East Coast inflection.

"Umm, okay, I'm sorry . . . I can come back if you'd like."

"No, do you want a hit?"

"What is that?"

"It's dope."

"I know it's dope, but that thing, what is it?"

"It's a bong. Man, this is going to be an interesting year," Enrico said and took another long, slow hit. "By the way, when I run for office in ten years, if you mention this to any one, I'll have you killed." He paused for full dramatic effect. "I'm not fucking kidding you."

Stephen smiled and sat on the edge of his bed. He looked at the white tiles of the drop ceiling, at the black-and-gray asbestos-tiled floor, at the gray cinder block walls, at the pile of pornographic magazines Enrico had piled in the corner by his bed; anything to avoid making eye contact at this man-boy seated across from him. Stephen's head was hurting and there were tears welling at his eyes, which he gamely fought back. What am I doing here? I don't belong here, I don't belong here, I don't belong here. His stomach churned at the condescending manner, no, it was downright boorish behavior, of his new roommate. Still, as the sweet-smelling smoke floated out of Enrico's bee-stung lips and into Stephen's nostrils, Stephen desired to join in. In his romantic mind, he was in the red velvet opium den of Sherlock Holmes, or the cold-water flat of a young John Coltrane, or seated on a hill overlooking the rusted boxcars of a San Francisco freight yard at sunset. Stephen Darden, honor student, immigrant son and good boy, was dissolving into a memory only as real as the wisps of smoke that rose before him.

A Day at the Races

Colin wrapped his blue windbreaker around his thin waist; the sun was too damn hot and there was no wind getting through the grandstand. The first race had just finished, and Colin had gotten there too late to bet on it. He had to return home and take a nap after this morning's chemo, even though he made a promise to himself he wouldn't let this goddamn thing get in the way of his schedule. A horse named "Better Days" came in dead last as he filled out his slip and slid it under the thick Plexiglas.

Goddamn right . . . Better Days, but not for you, old gal, he laughed to himself. Hopefully, for me, he mumbled half aloud.

He stood, shading his eyes with the racing form, and the sun flowed down like honey and warmed his pale, sagging skin. There weren't too many folks here for the Thursday afternoon races; the day-shift boys wouldn't be here until the middle of the third race. Damn shame, Colin thought, to be stuck inside, building cars, on a beautiful day like today. It's been two years for me. Two brilliant years not on the clock. Too much television, though, not enough racing. Not enough fishing either. Why haven't I been fishing lately? Oh yes, two children finishing high school and college, that's what. And me trying to be the good house-husband while Fiona works two jobs, God bless her. Ah, I did my time, that's sure enough. Worked two jobs for twenty years. Three jobs when we first came across, barely enough time to take a piss and pass out before I had to be to the print shop or the store, and then back to the hotel, or was I working at the hospital then? Jesus Christ, I've had more jobs than a Mexican. Back-breaking, every one of them. Cleaning puke off the bathroom wall, or shit out of a sink—what kind of person shits in a sink? What kind of person cleans up after someone who shits in a sink? Someone who likes to eat, I reckon. Not the shit! Someone who doesn't want their kids to have to do the same kind of piss-poor work as their old man, that's who. It wasn't as bad as all that, it was only a few years, right, old man? Lots of poor saps do that sort of thing their entire lives. Poor, poor, pitiful saps.

Then a familiar voice calls out, breaking him out of this lamentation. He thought it was Jimmy B. at first, but then when the man got closer, he realized it was Jimmy's brother, Mikey. The two were almost identical, even though Jimmy was two years younger and had blonde hair. But they both usually were wearing their Ford baseball caps, so you had to wait until they got close enough to tell for sure.

"Mikey B., skipping out a bit early, are we? Not that I blame you on a beautiful day like today."

"Nah, I just skipped out on stopping at the Derby for a frosty cool beverage. I was feeling too goddamned lucky."

"Not as lucky as me, my boy, not as lucky as me."

"What are you so lucky for? You getting a little extra from old Fiona darling?"

"Jesus, no, not even close to that. I can't explain what it is, Mikey, it's just that I woke up with a feeling, a good, good feeling. You ever get those feelings, you just got to trust them."

"Sounds like you found Jesus or something, buddy boy."

"Nah, it wasn't Jesus . . . that old bunch of . . . I don't know . . . maybe it's Jesus, maybe he's speaking to me in some sort of special prophecy. Telling me to enjoy the beautiful sunshine and bet on the ponies. I'll betcha Jesus would have been a great lover of the track. He was so kind and gentle to all sorts of bums like us, and of the whores too.

"Speaking of that, did you get a load of that number over there? Is she Puerto Rican? God damn, I'd eat all that and come back for seconds. I'd have me a whole genuine, all-you-can-eat buffet. Damn."

"Always the ladies' man. I'm sure she'd love to hear your sweet talk. Why don't you go make an offer?"

"Maybe after the next race. Hey, you got a smoke?"

"Sorry, my boy. No smokes. I gave it up."

"You quit? Son of a bitch. I never thought I'd live to see the day old Colin the chimney calling it quits on the cancer sticks. What gives?"

"Nothing really. I just decided I don't want to waste the goddamn money. Think of all the extra cash I can invest here, make my money do a little work for me, for a change."

Colin decided not to tell him about the cancer, or the book he started writing this morning, or that he had indeed said a rosary this morning before going to St. Margaret's for his chemo, and that there was indeed a peacefulness that fell upon him when he was finishing the third decade. Instead, they stood in the bright sunshine on this Michigan summer day and laughed when their horses came in, and cursed when they lost it all on the next race. It was just better this way.

Still Photograph—Ezra Pound, Playing Tennis

Voice over, thin and high-pitched.

"When he came to visit me in Rapallo, he really came to beg for money. He started, of course, asking about my ideas. About my insights on the world economic situation and what we could do to get some of the better ideas about the gold standard over to that bastard Roosevelt and his boys. Some folks are just so thick-headed it makes one's head absolutely swim. Anyways, I told him that there is no way the dolts in America are going to give a rat's ass about this Bloom character, but that should not stop him. And he should definitely not, not, not, not, not, accept Mr. Fjord's request to give training speeches to the assembly line workers. Although, Mr. Fjord's idea to educate the mindless masses was impressive, it would certainly ruin any chance Joyce had of getting himself a position in the Mussolini government, which he keeps on yippering on and on about. I lent him some cash and got him drunk."

Medium Shot of Dr. Ignatius T. Smiley, Professor Emeritus, Xavier University

"What people don't realize is that at this time, Joyce was revered in such a way that few writers could have dreamed of. He was almost like a rock star, or an actor on a soap opera, or perhaps like an athlete. This was before his Carnegie Hall performance, which created the legend that we know today, but still, in capital cities in Europe at this time, Mr. Joyce could not go unrecognized. One time, he was dining with a female acquaintance in Trieste and a mob of schoolgirls came up and tried to rip his clothes off. It was unseemly and unheard of at the time. His books just stirred such a strong visceral reaction from people, especially from the easily impressionable youth of the modern generation, that they simply could not control themselves, their humours being so aroused. Few people realize that he took to wearing the eye patch as an effort to blend in to his surroundings, to be more inconspicuous in crowds; they were almost as commonplace as hats in more fashionable quarters. Another area very few people know about involves Mr. Fjord's clandestine overtures to Mr. Joyce's to become affiliated with Fjord Auto Company as a corporate trainer. Mr. Fjord had long been a proponent of advanced education for all people, especially for those people on his assembly line. He realized early on that simply providing a wage for his people was not enough. He felt a moral responsibility to cultivate their intellects as well. Who better to help him in this endeavor than the most popular writer in Europe, a place Mr. Fjord often looked to for inspiration?

Introducing Mr. Black

It was about 10:30 P.M. on Tuesday night and I was just getting ready to brush my teeth and head up to bed when the phone rang. It was Stephen. His speech was rapid and high-pitched; he talks that way when he was excited.

"David, guess what? Well, I've got some good news. That guy I was telling you about, that producer, Mr. Black, he sounds interested. I mean interested. He still wants to see a script before totally saying yes, but . . . but it sounds like he is definitely interested . . . . His family is from County Clare . . . . He was an English Lit major undergrad, then this and that happened and he ended up in law school."

"But he likes the story, I mean, he thinks it's good?"

"Oh yeah, a documentary about James Joyce. I mean, we have a pretty good slant on things, don't you think?"

"Yeah, oh I mean I think it's great, but you know me . . . He didn't think it's too . . . ummm . . . what's the word I'm looking for . . . marginalized?"

"Well, he had a few ideas for script changes, but . . . you know . . . just to make it a bit more mainstream, give us a shot at public television . . . but nothing really that would affect the integrity of the story."

"Did he like the title? What'd he say about it?"

"He loved it . . . I mean, who wouldn't? *JJ's Eyes*, it's so . . . it almost sounds like it could be a Tricia Gomez song, or K-Dogg feeling romantic. The kids will love it. Look, JJ is already the bomb, we just have to be true to the story and everybody will be going nuts for it. And Black had tons of really great ideas for marketing tie-ins, locations, and casting . . ."

"Casting, what do you mean? It's a documentary . . ."

"Well, right, of course, but . . . you know, it's all about making it true . . ."

"Making it true with actors . . ."

"Look, wasn't it Joyce who said, 'art is the lie that tells the truth?'"

"Umm . . . I don't think that was him . . ." But for the life of me, I couldn't remember who said that, or something similar to that.

"David, my *amigo* (I hated when he spoke Spanish like that), relax (I hated when he told me to relax). It will all work out. We'll have plenty of time to talk later. Hey, do you guys want to meet for drinks later?"

"Aww man, it's after ten, I'm going to bed soon. I got to get up for work and be at full functioning to sit in my cube in the basement of the Albert Cohn building, and process important documents for semi-indigent retarded people all day, and I don't just mean my clients (ba-da-bum)."

"I thought you said a monkey could do your job."

"Yeah, but for now, I'm the monkey."

In real life, we continued gibbering for a while, but for full artistic impact, I will stop the conversation with that last, very clever line of mine. I always felt satisfied when I was able to come up with a line that evoked the witty banter of any number of mediocre sitcoms from the seventies. You can almost hear the "laugh" light pulsing on after the last syllable of monkey fades away. I hope you can hear it too. You may want to adjust your volume control, if this did not.

Liz's Notebook, Page 27

The light was orange and danced on our faces and our tongues.

We were young and dumb, about to come undone, So we lied, so we lied.

Sung softly, almost like a whisper. Acoustic guitar strummed lightly. E minor, then A minor.

The chorus:

> And when I fall into your eyes
> I always die, I always die.
> G, no, not hopeful enough.
> D, that might work.

The opening song?

This is really going to happen, I think. I never really trusted Stephen, but it sounds like he's really going to pull through this time. Dave says this Mr. Black helped start *Little America Films* . . . Although he's not with them now, for some reason . . . There's something going on with my belly. I either have a tumor or I'm pregnant. I hope I don't die before the movie comes out.

Standing in the shower, thinking

Stephen thought of the ink on his father's hands. Down in the bowgees. Ass-high in snot. Slower. The hum and grind of metal upon himself. The mind never gets used to a lot. Don't forget to breathe. Lathering of the shampoo—God, that feels good. I wonder if I'd be dead if we hadn't moved to America? Cousin Bobby, blown to bits in Belfast, 1983. Paulie put in prison for five years for blowing up the MP's car, without the goodly man in it, of course. Paulie was no murderer. He just wanted to send a message. Why is it up to me to live out the American dream? Fame. Fortune. TV guide. The water cascading down his shoulders and back. Big boobs and blonde hair. God Bless America. Angelina breathing like a cow on the satin sheets beside me, needing to have her tummy rubbed to fall asleep and keep away the bogeyman. "Sleeping Habits of the Young and Nearly Famous," that'd make a great television show. The spit coalescing on the lip, the morning hair, the stink breath—how could we get the viewer to understand this? Huh? And with all the technology we have, you'd think we could at least do this. It's not like I'm asking for a cure for cancer. He turned the nozzle off and stood for a second, listening to the water being sucked down the drain and watching it swirl. They say it swirls in the opposite direction in the southern hemisphere. Which direction is that again? Counterclockwise, I suppose. Righty tighty, lefty loosey. I wonder if I could stay in here all day?

A Rough Cut

They, we, you, were sitting four in the living room in Chicago. Stephen, the zero, smiling, red-haired and red-faced from the heat. Richard, the Anglican with the slender ears and all, almost elfish, was drinking warm tap water to clear his intestines. Me and Liz, sitting, holding hands, blind to what was happening, the still warmth of the marriage carrying us forward on some river, floating atop the waves.

"What does your dad think about doing this?" Liz asked.

"He seems to be enjoying it. I think it's good for him. It gives him something to do during the day, now that he can't go to the track or the bar. Jinny says he practices reading each page three or four times before he presses the record button," Stephen said.

"That's something. I can't think of having the patience to actually sit down and do something like that. Just do it over and over until you get it right, and then how do you ever know it's right? I mean, I think I would think about all the ways you could do it and should do it, and think about the perfect way and just not do it. I think that's why I'm so successful at being an unpublished writer," I said.

"That, and your writing is bad," Richard said.

I shot him a dirty look.

"Well, when I was doing that stupid hemorrhoid commercial, the director was going for this one shot—me running into the bathroom with a look of extreme discomfort on my face. This one shot we did like fifteen or twenty times. It was like three seconds in the commercial. It took ten hours. It took a crew of six people ten hours to get three seconds of film for a commercial to sell a hemorrhoid relief cream, can you believe that?" Stephen said.

"It's pretty easy to believe, just turn on the news . . . the world is one big hemorrhoid," I said.

"What I wonder is, I mean, it's great that you're following your dream and acting and that, and that you're actually getting work, but do you ever sit there and think, I have a master's degree from Harvard and I'm trying to get this ridiculous commercial? I mean, do you ever want to go back to school?" Liz asked.

Stephen looked away from her and towards the window, at the sunlight dying before him. His lips quivered, almost imperceptibly. He scratched the back of his head. "Of course, of course. Almost everyday, I think about it. Maybe I will, one day. But I think about everything that's going on right now. I think of this movie, of my dad dying and him knowing he's dying, and still him sitting down on that stupid brown chair and reading the book and practicing the words, and everyday him finding some sort of strength to press play . . ."

Richard put his hand on Stephen's shoulder. Liz looked at me and I knew she felt awful about bringing the subject up, but she realized an apology was an unsavory salve at this point. Still, she tried.

"Stephen, I am so sorry . . . I didn't mean it to sound that way . . . I didn't . . ." she said.

He smiled and wiped the corner of his eye. "I know, I guess I'm just a little touchy about this whole 'life is a meaningless pile of shit' notion these days . . ."

"That slogan, my friend, would be perfect for a promo poster for our film," Richard said.

Stephen chuckled a bit and the mood lightened. He reached over for the play button and we watched the next scene of Colin Darden reading pages 243-245, his voice thin and wheezy, struggling to maintain an even rhythm. It didn't really matter how he sounded, I figured. Glancing over at Stephen staring intently at his father's image on the screen, I knew that he never wanted the book to end, thinking maybe that Colin's life was no longer measured in days or hours, but in words and pages.

Richard's Napkin, Denny's, Westville, Michigan.

There are many points of view.
None depend on you!
As the grimace fades from a faceless age, and we all grow cold, old, alone, together. in a violent electron storm we are born! Hooray today!
How do you live a dead language? David asks.
The scene shifts to a cobblestoned street in Belfast, Sarajevo, Port-au-Prince, Tunis, Belize, Detroit. A young, red-haired boy bounces a ball. You watch it bounce and bounce and bounce, and then you notice the smoke and fire from the automobile burning in the fuzzy background.
The scene shifts to a white-tiled kitchen in Dearborn—The HOMETOWN OF HENRY FORD! A brown-haired woman in a green housedress, with a yellow apron, screams and lunges to tackle her young daughter as flames engulf the toddler's loose, yellow, cotton nightgown. The daughter reaches for her mother's teakettle atop the stove. Trying to help. To be the big girl. The big sister. Helping momma. Third degree. The flesh of the fleshless. The flesh of the innocents rolling on the kitchen floor. The slow motion of the horror of the sickening smell and gut screaming of the mother and the daughter, limp in her arms, and the daughter breathing beneath the weight of gravity, and the air evacuates her body and the sick, sick smell of flesh, which should never be burned.
The scene shifts—it is night—a gunshot. One.

The scene shifts—it is day—sunlight. Outside shot—the Mediterranean, on an island where nothing happens. A man scratches his long, gray beard. He is tan and well rested and he is reading a clever mystery novel about a priest. He has no desire to return home.

I see you with my x-ray eyes.

Home is a long way away.

Your stomach is cancer but your soul will rise.

Title Cards, Simple Black Lettering on Ivory-colored Parchment Paper:

Ulysses,
A heroic journey, with film, etc.
Voice Over—Liz's Voice—Soft and Slow
Words Scroll Across the Screen as She Reads.
"As the lines increase, their impact decreases.

My skin is changing before me.
Lines, leather and sags.

I am weak under the burden of words, smother
    cover yet I breathe
A benevolent reprieve.
Heaven breeze cools and smoothes me.
It is not destiny, but divinity."
Recently Discovered Notebook of James Joyce,
    Dated 1919.

Antics and Semantics

Richard put his arm around me at the restaurant and said, "I got it on film."

I looked at him blankly. "You got what on film?"

"The service, the eulogy, the whole thing right here, I got it," and he held up a digital camera.

I was pissed off at his brazen opportunism, so I said, "I wouldn't actually call that 'film,' would you? It seems like you captured it to digital or caught it on disk, or whatever you say about it, but I'm pretty sure it's not 'film.'"

"Screw you. I got it. I got it and it's going to be in the movie."

I was pretty tired and drunk by this point and hadn't been to a funeral in many years since I was a teenager, and I felt foggy headed and thick-bellied, and didn't feel like talking or even thinking about this stupid movie.

"Great, that's great. You're a real sweet boy, Richie, Ricardo, and I hope you become everything you deserve to be."

"What the hell is that supposed to mean?"

"It means just what I said it means. What do you think, that it means something else or something? Like it has multiple meanings? I'm not smart like you, Dickie boy, I can't think so cleverly."

"I suppose you're right. I thought I was talking to one of my friends who graduated from Michigan, not one that got kicked out."

"I did not get kicked out, you sonofabitch. I left of my own accord. I left because I was not satisfied with my educational experience there. A whole bunch of phony-baloneys."

"Phoneys? Is that right, Holden Caulfield? Was you're experience at the community college much more authentic then?"

"At least, the people were honest. They were real people. Just like the people we grew up with, just like we used to be. I mean, do you even know who you are anymore? Because I sure as hell have no clue who you are or who I am, or who any of us are." I knew I had gone too far down John Hughes territory, but I couldn't help it.

Richard smiled at the end of my diatribe. He put his hand on my shoulder and said, "Davey, you're right. I'm sorry. Maybe this whole thing just has my emotions up. Why am I such an asshole at times?"

He was right, he really could be an asshole, but I was being the bigger asshole, and I didn't have the cajones to own it, so I just didn't say anything. We stood in an awkward silence until an old friend from high school came over and rescued us with the mindless tedium of "catching up."

Liz Walks.

Exterior shot. She stands at the bottom of a large stone staircase, up a lush, green hillside. There are fountains of water shooting into the air on either side, forming an archway. She is wearing a black cocktail dress. Barefooted. The fountains are choreographed with the music. Their movement is her movement.

Music: Faure's *Requiem*

The stairs are stone and broken before her. We are still as she moves away from us beneath the fountain of water. If we were not so afraid, we would know the water is blood and Liz will never die. There is a building at the top of the stairs that looks vaguely familiar to us. I so desperately want it to be her home, her sanctuary, a place of safety. Her dress is black and elegant, and I can see the faces of the butterfly powder flying off it. The stuff on the wings. The powder. Yes. Yes.

She is almost to the top of the stairs and the music is so sad now. I hope this party won't be a bore. All politico and dead poet. All Yankee Doodle. All hippy hip. I hope there will be hyacinths and freesia and hydrangeas strewn about the marble floor. I hope their will be mangoes and kiwi flowing off the tables. There will be a fire in the fireplace that gives only light, not heat. I hope my grandmother is there with a piece of apple pie and cheddar cheese.

I am older now, and looking back, the colors seem brighter now. The blues and the reds are all fire or super lasers together. I wish she would turn and come back down the stairs, where I am standing. Waiting for her. I know she must have left me. But I did not know it would be so painful. She walks so gracefully, doesn't she? Just like a young bride, a young mother. The stairs are soft beneath her feet, as if she is simply floating. I am older now and I know that people have miracles inside of them. Locked inside. I have never seen them, but I believe that they are there. Inside of them are miracles. If I did not believe in them, then I would have never made this film for you.

    She is at the top of the stairs and my hands are trembling with excitement and fear now. But you can tell that, can't you? Surely, you can at least see that. I have written that she will stop at the top of the stairs, turn, and wave at me. She knows to count to fifteen, then turn and walk to the small stone building at the top. Is it a church? Is it a cottage? Why can't I remember what I wrote? It seems essential that she understand her destination. I am sure I wrote it down, we must have spoken about it, yet I have no memory of where she will end up. We have rehearsed this scene every morning in our gray apartment, with the man upstairs banging on the pipes. We have practiced this every Sunday morning as we knelt in sorrow and in hope. The goodly friars of St. Francis splashed our faces in the cleansing water of our baptism. The gentle and goodly Fr. Matt, thin and young, like a big brother, "God is good." And we with our *Great Amen's* Knowing this, knowing this, but still . . . And the smell of the incense on this day, hovering above the brazier, sending our prayers to God in heaven, through the green Pewabic tile and the gold-painted ceiling, through the sky above Washington Boulevard and the stink of the almost dead city into God's waiting nostrils, where he will inhale our prayers and know them to be ours. He is like the Great Mother Bear who knows her cubs. He will know us too. He will lead us away from the fiery shores and into the cold waters of Lake Michigan, where we will sleep peacefully in the frigid blue. Otto, the ex-philosophy professor, and current homeless man, sleeps in the pew next to us, his face caked with the grime of the modern city streets (untouched by Nebuchadnezzar), feces under his fingernails, grease on his gray beard, the acrid smell of urine wafting in with the incense. God will surely know this son. And we pray for Otto to find some place warm to sleep on this too-cold October night. And we thank God for Otto's husky baritone, reading a passage from the

Gospel of Matthew, and Otto thanking God for being called to serve Him. And I still feel ashamed for envying my friends' SUV and cable TV. I squeeze Liz's hand and pray to God that I have the strength to keep breathing.

The music stops suddenly and we become aware of the silence that is around us.

Slow fade out.

David Gets in Trouble

We all write our lives in poems of bones, oil, and ash. The words are dissonant in design. All history is bunk, my Temporama is a piece of junk. Three brake jobs, rubber molding, peeling off the driver's side, air conditioner out, seat belt out, transmission out, three years old and with regular oil changes to boot!

Now ten years old and with 169,000 miles—thanks to my father's almost Christlike ability to resurrect transmissions and radiators from the tomb of Stanley's Junkyard off of Michigan Avenue.

Did Xeno drive half the distance in an auto?

Hence, paralysis?

Did Paul stone Stephen in an auto?

Dresden firebombs—auto?

London calling in an auto?

The Joads autoed in irony, not destiny.

The Kennedys shall be omitted, for once; they deserve at least that.

We took the train to Philadelphia and stood where Washington once stood and smiled and saluted at the Japanese tourists. How did our country survive? My family can't even agree on what to order at McDonald's. We took photographs of each other and goofed around, making funny faces with our tongues out.

Circe's auto was in the shop when I arrived with my wife. We were not uninvited.

It is a red auto, the Tempo, rounded somewhat at the ends,

but not too much. For those of you reading this 263 years from now, an automobile is a primitive mode of transportation. It is for thugs and ruffians and yahoos. Nothing is great or small except by comparison, except for the auto—it just sucks. Do not forgive us out of pity—we knew what we were doing. We loved every minute of it. All motor here and motor, motor, there everywhere a moto-motor.

Every minute of everyday in Metropolia, those autos, those cars flip right over on the roads, killing the driver and passengers—usually babies unfastened in the back seat. The traffic slows and we crane our necks to see the carnage. Traffic becomes congested, but if we are lucky, we see a decapitated woman! Callooh callay! Henry Ford was a Nazi sympathizer and we worship him like a freaking god! He never played quarterback on the high school football team, and neither did Thomas Alva Edison, for that matter. I refuse to pay money to see his stupid house any more.

The best and the brightest among us
(to the tune of "Did you Evah?").

R: (in Chicago) Yes, the bread was delicious.
Me: (in Dearborn, the birthplace of Henry Ford) So, you enjoyed it?
R: Oh yes, it was great. Just great.
Me: Good.
R: Yeah, hey, I started the genetic thing.
Me: On the web? It will be obsolete in ten years.
R: Ten years is forever. It will be obsolete in three.
Me: So will we.
R: We already are. We won't even be a mem-o-ry.
Me: At least we'll be free.
R: Can't be free if we've never been trapped.
Me: We're ultimately trapped, merely as men.
R: Neo-Nietzsche bullshit crap.
Me: We must remember the ghosts among us.
R: Such a luxury.

Me: We must celebrate the dead within us.
R: A waste of industry. More psycho lingua polit babble.
Me: I'm at home among the rabble!
R: Goodbye, my brother, did you evah?
Me: Ta-ta, I nevah!

7.35 A.M., 28 July, 1997

The gas pedal is to the floor as I accelerate onto the exit ramp, desperate to reach at least sixty miles per hour to avoid being rear-ended by a gravel hauler, going at least seventy-five miles per hour in the right lane during morning rush hour. How do people even live through a single day? The Tempo strains and rattles, but she makes it, and we ease through the flashing yellow at Trumbull.

I notice some sort of commotion ahead of me. There is a yellow plastic bag that hangs from a junk maple tree and I'm driving slowly by it, not sure exactly what it is that I am seeing. The bag is large and looks like a body bag, except it is yellow. I think it is a body bag, but then chastise myself for having such an overactive imagination. There are six cop cars parked on the street, facing in every direction. Two cops are on the street, standing by the yellow bag hanging from the tree. The other cops are talking and drinking coffee in their car. They don't have any expressions on their faces and they're all just sort of there, not really moving or doing much of anything. I drive by slowly, thinking for sure it was not a man in a yellow plastic bag but a bunch of garbage or dead cats left from the frat boys or something. So I go to work and I forget about it.

It's not in my mind at all.

Later that night, I hear on the radio that the police have found a body by the campus and they're treating it like a homicide. Right there on the football field. The man was in his early forties. The name and race of the man and the cause of death was not stated on the radio.

I do not feel transformed.

The next day, I'm at lunch at the Tiny Village Café just off of Cass, sipping decaffeinated green tea, waiting for my sweet potato jerk. I'm talking about the president's racial initiative experiment with some co-workers, who happen to be African-American. I happen to be not African-American, as you know. Anyway, this guy who went to school in the 1960s at Indiana University, of all places, was telling me about all the protests and the trouble on campus and all that. I say I thought that stuff only happened at Berkeley and Ann Arbor, and maybe once at Harvard. He didn't laugh but just shifted his toothpick, so I knew what he was getting at.

He starts telling me this story: "So anyway, I was leaving my apartment. Maybe four or five blocks from campus. Anyway, I'm leaving my apartment to head for breakfast and this beat-up brown van pulls up slowly in the parking lot. The door slides open and out jump a couple of guys wearing army fatigues and black berets. They got shotguns and they just blow away these fat-ass white cops just standing on the corner. Just blew them away with shotguns right there on the corner, boom, boom! Loud as hell. And the blood just sprayed out, I swear to you. Then these guys walk back to the van, get in and the van pulls away. It was some crazy times then. So you think this country's got a racial problem? You bet your white ass, it does."

He chuckles and says, "Man, those were some fucking crazy times."

29 July 1997

Nothing about the guy in the yellow bag hanging from the tree on the radio. I forced myself to buy both of the local papers and watch the evening news to see if I can find out more about this dead man in a yellow bag hanging from the tree. The quietness has my X-files all riled up and I begin to suspect conspiracy. Clearly, the university is stifling this to not freak out the commuters (racial buzz word).

While watching television, I wonder whose generation am I.

The big news is the SuperNews news crew faked an ambulance run to prove that metro area drivers do not slow down when they hear the siren. Apparently, people keep driving, go faster, and even flip off the ambulance drivers despite the wailing sirens and flashing lights. For some reason, they do this at 11:06 P.M. on a minor street and the one car on the road actually does pull over. Obviously, it's a total bust, even though they build it up like it's the next athlete sex/death scandal.

And then the breaking news of some local Detroit cop serving up Daddy-o in the big house finds out he's doing more time, not by his wife, or his lawyer, but the news crew! They walk into the gray, cinderblock-walled prison meeting room, with the camera rolling and the portly, mustachioed newsman says in a thunderous voice, "Jason Topinski, have you talked to your lawyer?"

He shakes his pale face, "No."

"We have some news that you might want to know. Mr. Topinski, your appeal has been denied. You must remain in prison for the remainder of your term."

Mr. Topinski begins blubbering.

"Mr. Topinski, can you tell our viewers how you are feeling right now?"

Mr. Topinski can't speak.

"You seem upset right now, do you have anything to tell our viewers?"

He chokes out between sobs, "I love you, Rita. I love you, little Jason." He stares directly at the camera as if he can see his family back home, sitting in their small living room, hugging each other and weeping for their lost father.

All this news caught on videotape for our viewing enjoyment.

But that's not all. A quick cut-away to the news lady on a remote site, where this whole motorist beating incident occurred. There is no moon this night, but the camera's light is bright and it's shining out into the street. You can see the shadows it casts.

Suddenly, you hear a tire squeal and a thump, and then a dog yelping and whining. The lady winces and says, "Excuse me, but a dog has just been hit by a car in the street behind me," but she finishes her reporting because she's a professional.

I want to watch the made-for-TV movie to find out how it turns out! People really say that after their neighbors have been killed. They really get sucked into this weird MIT anti-reality thing and they are all just nuts. I mean, *Brave New World* is mild compared to this stuff. And *Fahrenheit 451* is just a quaint bedtime story.

The point is, it's been over a year and he's still dead. And this film, this story, whatever it is we are doing to try to figure this thing out, it just has me feeling all crabby. It's like I'm just thinking about everything all the time, and the more I think, the more I realize just how nuts it all is, and I feel like I'm sixteen and riding that train to New York again and not twenty-five and trying to live a life.

Why don't you try writing/acting/filming/singing/etc?
Me: Not everything is a mask.
Parenthesis: Only my pen knows the difference.
We would move to Paris if we had any _____.

1. Money
2. Friends
3. Guts
4. Fear

There is no fear, only fear.

The camera circles above them.

The four are seated around a table. There is hummus, mjadra, and pita bread in Styrofoam boxes on the table. The table is cluttered with food and elbows and laughter, and two almost-empty bottles of Merlot.

If you listen closely, you think you hear *Giant Steps* far way. Cut to close-up of Stephen.

Stephen
Okay, okay, here's one—*The Swingers*. Four guys from Toledo move to Zaire to open a gay bar for pygmies. They own only one Michael Jackson album and they teach the pygmies all the moves to *Thriller*. Then one day, one comes down with a weird virus and the other three are murdered by rebel troops.

The four burst out laughing.

Richard
Four words—"My mother, my Latin teacher."

David
No Existen genio sine algo dementia!

They cheer and toast.

Stephen
Okay, okay, here it is, there's this killer mime.

They all boo.

David.
No mimes. We all agreed, Stephen. No goddamn mimes.

Stephen
Okay, okay. He's an ex-mime. Who writes only haikus.

Liz
Is he gay or straight?

Stephen
Very straight. He is super-straight.

David
White or African-American?

Stephen
We don't know at this point. We'll test it, test it and see what works, you know. Anyway, one day, he finds a lost puppy and he befriends it because he's an ex-mime and he's sensitive, you know. He goes around and recites these poems as the dog barks out the meter. The meter of the poem.

David
I love it. Stephen, it's beautiful. We'll get that British guy to be the mime—well, the ex-mime. The haikuist.

Richard
Or is haikuer?

Liz
It's lee Man Haiku man, and his dog. Catchy, dontcha think?

Stephen
I was thinking more like Stiv, the Haiku Dude.

Richard
He should do it all from inside a box in a cart that the dog pulls along throughout the city.

Stephen
It'd have to be a pretty big dog. Do you think we can afford it? Such a big dog.

Richard
We can afford it. A retriever, not a Lab, but with make-up, no one would be able to tell. Besides, it would just make the whole thing work.

Stephen

I don't know. Maybe it's not such a good idea. I mean the whole ex-mime-poet-with-a-dog thing, it's so trendy now. There were like two or three at Sunsplash last year alone.

Richard

No. No way. It's classic. It's a classic theme. It's Don Quixote, its Dante and his sidekick, Virgil. It's Abraham and Isaac. It's all in there, it's all in that box with the mime and the big, beautiful dog, Stephen. Can't you just feel it, man? It's all in that box.

Liz

I think it should be a real Labrador. They are so well-shaped. Or wait, wait, wait. Wait a minute. The dog, an IRISH SETTER. They nod and laugh as they have a mutual epiphany—a mupiphany.

Stephen

We'll test it. We'll see. Maybe this will work.

Fade out.

* * *

Colin, Home from the Races

His skin dull-gray and sagging from his brittle frame. I'm ready for a goddamned drink. Detroit stink and cowards, worse than the riots. The knife, the fire underneath the ribcage. Visualize white. Nothing. Goddamn idiot quacks. I hunger the blue death. Skull bugger, lisping nutbugger, dirt bag. Get me a GODDAMN DRINK!

His mother knew he would die this way. Quivery and like a sheep on the cold cave floor, with deep-red, invisible blood flooding his insides. Caught in the euphoria of tumors. The wind. Japanese ministers on holiday. Smoking $5.00 cigars like its opium gold dust. Watching the kiddies gyro and spiral on plastic tabletops. Throwing Scotch and vomit on taut flesh. I'm ready for a drink.

I am no man island no land no stand unplanned distand no land a land Island Island is planned no man no man no man

I am no man I am no man no man no man nomad I have no home I am not home I am not home nome nome nome nome NO NO NO NO NO NO NO NO!

Music: Static from the A.M. radio for at least twenty minutes.

His face is pale and wrinkled. He is seated on the red sofa. His wife is away at work. His son and daughters are away some place. He is alone. He sits alone. And he contemplates his pain of tumor. His impending death. Just the fear of it all and the loneliness. That is what I'm trying to get at here. The loneliness of the death and the pain. If I repeat it long enough, it will become meaningless to you. The pain and the lonely moment when one contemplates the death. The pain of living and mostly of dying. This is called "repetition," and it loses its impact and soon, you will not associate the words on the page with anything. It will not remind you of your own life and your own dead father. It will not remind you of your own tumor and your own impending death. It will not remind you of pain. You will snidely say to yourself that the only thing that is painful is reading this. This is just a book. This is just words of pain on the pain. On the pain. The loneliness of the page. It's just going to be noise, the pain, and the pain will just be noise, it will be nothing to you, it is just static. At some point, you will start to become very irritated and you will want to smash something up because your skin is just crawling on fire from the sheer annoyance of reading this. The pain and loneliness of dying are still inside you and the pain is not ever far away; it's in your rods and the pain is in your cones. And you try to distract yourself with the memory of something but you are losing your vision and unable to focus on anything but the static and the noise of the pain, and you hate me, you hate the pain, and you start singing a song at the top of your lungs, "O YOU CAN'T HURRY LOVE, NO YOU'LL JUST HAVE TO WAIT!" but you are just more noise underneath the noise of the pain, and it's inside of you like a giant bunch of tumors in your gut and in your pancreas and in your liver and in your stomach and in your rectum and in your prostate, and the pain is inside of you, gnawing away any substance and leaving emptiness, the lonely emptiness of the death and the hole is your gut and it is the pain and you are pacing the floor and you are pounding the wall and you are still screaming and you are still screaming and then you sit

>still on the red
>sofa in the blue television light
>and the cells
>divide
>and the air
>lowers
>and your heart
>lowers
>and you can
>breath
>slowly
>with your heart again
>and there you are sitting
>and there is soft wind
>and waves washing over you
>warmly and warmly and warmly
>on your flesh
>and you're floating on the waves of the warm water
>washing over.

* * *

Blues and Blues

Professor Ignatius T. Smiley
"Joyce was quite an accomplished tenor. Part of his unwavering popularity was his ability to infuse popular music of the day into his literature. In fact, his 'James Jive' tour of 1933 was a hit in many European capitals, especially Berlin."

A musical number, cabaret style: a chorus line, leggy blondes, all wearing sequined eyepatches. An empty night club, lit candles and red silk roses on the table, white linen tablecloth. Very classy.

Stephen, wearing a simple black eyepatch, with a thin mustache. He looks thin in his white linen suit and black hat.

A jaunty, swingy tune—Benny Goodman:
He sings, warbling tenor:

> "The trees are not women
> I know this to be true
> yet beneath the sky, I am hungry
> beneath the sky, I am cold.
>
> Trumpet takes the chorus.
> Since St. Louis still demands
> faithful doxology
> since Martin Luther still commands
> faithful theology
>
> A big twirl, a kick, trombones punch it:
> I know the freaks are watching you!
>
> The sky divides the eyes
> between waking and something less,
> the skin requires autumn
> the skin requires sick flesh.

Another chorus:

> Since St. Peter still speaks
> in cancer
> since St. Clare still speaks
> in plagues,
>
> I know the freaks are watching you
> from the murky waters of space."

Big ending, Stephen on his knees. Rips off his eyepatch and throws it to one of the chorus girls, the red-haired one, who swoons on the downbeat into the arms of her compatriots.

The spotlight turns and shines directly into the camera. Fade out.

* * *

David's Family "Holiday"

When I was ten and chubby, we went to Philadelphia to see history. We drove a blue 1974 Buick Century straight through from Detroit at night to avoid traffic, construction, motels, scenery. My father quaffed Maxwell House from his rusty thermos. The rest of us all slept, my sister and I, unbuckled in the back seat, of course. It was about 150 degrees Fahrenheit when we arrived and we pulled up right in front of Independence Hall. I cant remember what street it is on—Walnut, maybe, or is it Chestnut? So he pulled up in front, in the street, turned on the hazard lights and we jumped out.

"Parking in the city is just too goddamn expensive. It'll be all right," he said as we shuffled in line with a horde of German tourists.

They were very tall and wore open-toed shoes that I was always too self-conscious to wear. We stood behind the rope and listened to the park ranger babble on about compromise, or some such fascist propaganda. This all occurred before the murderous attacks of September 11, so I apologize for sounding so snarky about one of our country's finest historical monuments. But I was just a kid, after all. I didn't really know better.

The German tourists kept asking questions about the effect of the Second Continental Congress on the development of the Marshall Plan, and the park ranger just sort of passed out and seemed to have some sort of epileptic fit.

Dad grabbed me and Janey by the hand and said, "Let's get out of here, this is going to be a real shit-kicker."

So we left and drove to Hershey Pennsylvania via some two-lane road through Lancaster County, almost running over some dirty Mennonite boy on a scooter. Let me clarify, he actually was dirty; he was caked in mud and had a pig in a basket on the back of the scooter. I did not mean to imply that his affiliation with the Mennonite culture imbued him with a degraded social status. I have nothing personally against any form of alternate religious lifestyle, as I myself am a practicing Roman Catholic, who are known throughout history to open-mindedly embrace diverse racial and ethnic groups. In fact, some of my best friends are actually Mennonites, or they would be, if I had any friends.

We did not ride any of the amusement park rides, but we did buy some chocolate at a Seven-Eleven in Hershey.

I think we drove within five or ten miles of Gettysburg, so Dad figured we could just as well check that one off the list too.

* * *

It's A Wonderful Life

David and Liz, with her hair all honey-coloured, up, revealing her beautiful neck, sat in Dominici's underneath the night and the hanging yellow moon. The cilantro wafted from the gazpacho and into their eager heads. They had come here to avoid parents and the memory of parents and the 8:00 A.M. phone calls from parents on a Saturday. Not Paris, to be sure. Not Mexico City. Not San Francisco, but still, somewhere is better than anywhere else.

David
Doesn't being here make you feel so . . . old?

Liz
(Pause) Not in a bad way though.

David

(slurping gazpacho) Look at that table over there. Kids, they're just kids. Look, she's not even old enough to drink.

Cut to young teenage girl pulling a bottle of beer from baggy jean pocket.

Liz

God, I am so glad I am past that. Aren't you, David? I feel like I know myself so much, well, I feel that every crisis is not the end of the world and that life is just some big puzzle that you can just think about and figure out. I'm glad I don't have to wear clothes like that. I can walk around in slippers and a housecoat all day if I want. Just smoking cigarettes and drinking martinis.

David

This conversation sounds like we're trapped in some really bad student movie.

Liz

Except that we're not freaks.

David

Yes, we are. We are freaks.

Liz

Well, we're the good kind of freaks. Freaky freaks.

David

I know what you mean. I'm sick of living in my parents' basement or in Richard's attic. I want a house. Some place of my own where I can put up paintings and knock out the wall and plant a garden and not have to listen to the Jimi Hendrix Experience at 3:00 A.M., you know. Unless I want to. But then, part of me just wants to drive out west again. Do you remember that? Driving all night through Arizona and the sky just endless stars. A blanket of stars covering us. And listening to "Zurich is Stained" and singing along and just . . .

Liz
And eating those burritos in San Diego.

David
Those damn burritos. God, what did we ever do without cilantro? I wonder.

Liz
I think cilantro was the secret ingredient in ambrosia.

David
Is that why Zeus was so . . . amorous?

Liz
How did the Greek culture flourish for so many years with gods like that? Get real. I never thought you should worship someone whose relationship with his wife is more screwed up than yours. It just seems like bad practice.

David
The Greeks were the greatest rationalizers in history. Everything they did was just excused away by these incredibly bizarre stories. I mean, eating your kids, what is up with that? Or falling in love with yourself and being fully aware that you are, but still just pining away for yourself? And what about having a bird eat out your liver everyday? What lesson would you possibly learn from all that?

Liz
What about hubris, though?

David
At least you got a cool story made up about you, I guess. It's more than you can say about anything nowadays. The best you

can hope for is a video from your deathbed that your grandkids might pop in for laughs on Christmas Eve.

Liz
We really should move away, David.

David
We've been saying that a long time. Where would we go?

Liz
Halifax.

David
Halifax? Canada? They don't make cars there, do they?

Liz
I think they just fish, I'm not really sure. We could start the Exile in Halifax Movement. The "Fax-expats." Think of the fun your biographers will have with that.

David
I've decided against the whole biography thing. They get too personal. I'm going to write a journal instead and read it into a cassette recorder using different voices for each of my friends. And I may authorize a Scandinavian film crew to interview my students, but that is it.

Liz
I can't wait to see it. I'm sure it will be fascinating.

David
Well, you won't actually be able to see it. You see, I'll mandate that they destroy the film once they are done shooting it.

Liz
I love it. I guess I'll just have to start paying attention to you while we're still married.

David

That might be nice for a change.

* * *

David, in a dark mood.

3 August 1997

The film is going nowhere. Nowhere. And I am thick in the middle of it. Lost in the dead center.

What did Dis say to Dante, which his fascist editor cut from the book? "Help! I've fallen and I can't get up!"

This is a strange place to be alone among the sarcasm. The sarcastic. The sacrificed. The sacred. The sarcophagus. The sacrosanct. The sack. The sack. The sacked. The sackers. The slackers. The freak. To be home among the freaks.

—O you can't be serious, Ingmar

—Yes, I can!

Water in the lapel-flower, and a pie in the face.

I love it when big people fall down.

Some people you just can't recall. There is just too much flowing out. I'm everywhere right now. In the kitchen, shoving my face in the butter dish. Running north on Greenfield at 1:00 A.M., chased by death in the guise of a 1984 Camaro. Scratching the itch on my thighs. I should open the window. And let out the air. Some people can't be called, and they should know it. They should not call you. Simple. Nothing vague or mysterious about it. It's just cold, hard facts. The ugly truth. It's just the way things are. It's the whole nine yards. The whole ball of wax, the whole kit and caboodle The big enchilada, the baby face, on the double ffccccckkkrrrrr. I'm saving my dirty words for your father. He loves them so: in the eyes. The more niggers and Jews and faggots and Pollacks and wops, the better. They're only words, hey, fuckface? The whole world is bathed in love, like ether. It takes a Yankee intellectual to tell us that. The root of the lie extends to him and winds its way through the dirt to the dirt-eaters and to the deaths of the murderous poet, John Donne, and to the death of the cabinet member's son. It's all so much posturing and chest thrust out.

I realize today that I do not mind losing in sports. I know that this is a significant character flaw and dear diary, you must promise not to tell anyone, especially Stinky Johnson and Lefty Peterson and Frank.

This is not to say that there is not worth in those books, those writers.

Evanston, 1971. Pink E. Vurgil, Epic Titus, and all the cowboys and all their mouths and all the things which occurred then. The sheer hatred of the word, the hatred of meaning while lusting for the AGENDA, lusting for the self, the word as shit as self all the while. But still, I am not that, that is not me. I think much too literally. This book is as simple as boy meets girl. That is the difference.

10.45 P.M. You're on the speakerphone. Click.

* * *

Everybody Should Start a Band, to paraphrase Bob Mould

Liz played guitar and sang and I played bass and sang in a punk band of no reputation or success that we still committed scads of time and money to, determined to be successful and influential, failing at both. Still, it probably kept me alive more times than I'd care to admit—living in my parents' basement, writing maudlin poetry, friendless. The last show we played, we drove home from Chicago, leaving Wicker Park at 3:00 A.M. after the gig. This takes on a significance if you're sixteen and in a rock band. Otherwise, it seems vaguely irritating. Upon reflection, it is nice not to have to use the word, "gig" with any frequency these days.

There are not really words, good reader, which can describe the combination of euphoria, lust, and shame that one feels after one has exposed one's creative heart on one's creative sleeve to a roomful of drunk kids wearing untucked flannel shirts and ripped jeans. Or having old Polish men with scruffy beards and crooked teeth swearing at you and threatening you with a bottle of Smirnoff. Of course, no one getting a bit of what you're all about. That is, your sensitive and poetic lyrics, bathed in irony and thick with allusions to other sensitive and ironic lyricists. This sensitivity is masked in the waves of distortion and feedback that you've cultivated to demonstrate your anger, and to hide the fact that you can't really play the guitar. So you're really just impotent and silly and you figure you may as well be a poet because then, you won't be so cigarette stinky. But you can't just be a poet, it has to be you, so you can now assume that you will be impotent at that as well. That's the vanity of the punk and the pop-culture purveyors. Every bit of drool is so significant. So meaningful and rhapsodic.

You've got to start asking yourself some serious questions if you're thirty years old and the only creative connection you can make is with the beating of a bass drum. Remember, David, it's not your heartbeat. ITS JUST A PERCUSSION INSTRUMENT.

In the film, we see:

The camera lens opens up and out pops a mustachioed Mexican cabinet member, wearing a blue pinstripe suit and a red silk tie with no visible pattern on it. He is very slender but not sickly. His eyes are round and look like dimes. You guess he's still depressed about the death of his son by John Donne, the poet serial killer. Above and around you is air, very warm, and we are sitting on wooden folding chairs. He is sobbing.

Tight shot on his foot, spotlighted.

Opening bars from Faure's *Requiem* are audible, as if on a scratchy Victrola.

It claws at your skin and enters you. The foot of the Mexican cabinet member taps softly in the white light. So out of sync with the music that I begin sobbing too. Stephen says something in Spanish and he begins sobbing too. Time thickens and oozes sludge over our foot and we can no longer hear the music. Our own sobbing, too, cannot be heard.

Don't you think we would go back to Chicago and Phil's Musical Café, if we could? Of course we would. We would be liars if we said we would not. At least we are not that. No, we are not liars. We had never meant to mourn the death of the cabinet member's son in a rest stop outside of Kalamazoo at 4:30 in the morning. Not even the semi-truck can be heard. Not the insect suicide. Not the whoring. Not the requiem on the gramophone. Only waves of white-light audio. It felt like we should speak or say a prayer or something. But we were all gutless in the sludge.

Voice Over:

Lawrence, Kansas seems so far away now.

I quit the band after we got home. Things had gotten too weird in the sleepless nights and Sudafed haze. Opening for The Mobs, headed by Enrico, Stephen's ex-roommate, was the worst and final insult. Enrico, fresh from graduating in the upper third of his class at Northwestern Law School, desiring drugs and women, chose rock and roll as a suitable hobby. His band, playing bright pop music with Farfisa organs, wearing matching suits and ties, was signed by an extremely cool independent record label and debuted at number two on the CMJ charts. Our third self-produced cassette tape sold approximately twenty-three copies, give or take. We were pretty excited to get the gig and figured it to be just total dumb luck. Enrico was typically smug and suave that evening. Smoking clove cigarettes and downing Manhattans by the bucket, but looking like a movie star. The place was packed and there were always three girls around his arm so I didn't have a chance to talk to him until after the show.

"Where's Stephen?" he asked.

"He's out of town, filming a commercial in Los Angeles," I said.

"More ass cream?" Enrico asked.

"I'm not sure what it's for . . ."

"Too bad about his dad . . . that must really suck."

"Yeah, it's been pretty hard, but you know Stephen, he always has such a positive attitude about things."

He just looked at me, taking a drag on his cigarette. He leered in the direction of Liz.

"I always thought you and Stephen might be gay lovers or something. I guess I was wrong."

"Yeah, I guess so. If you're done being insulting, can I have our take?"

"Your take? What makes you think you're getting any cash? How many people came to see your cute little band? Two? Three? You know, you really are as bad as Stephen said you were. Don't quit your day jobs." He gave me a wad of cash and walked away.

I was pissed but was never good at snappy comebacks to tall, lanky, beautiful people, so I grabbed my guitar case and headed to the Tempo and Liz, waiting outside.

"Steve and Troy just split back to Stephen's apartment. So, what'd we get?"

"I don't know . . . I didn't count it. It seems like a lot," I said, showing her the thick wad of bills.

"Here, let me count it." She began thumbing through the bills—all ones, with a stash of monopoly money inside—twenty-five bucks total. "What the hell—"

I told her about my little discussion with Enrico. Her face turned red and she stomped over to the doors and pulled on them. They didn't budge, locked. She began pounding on the glass doors and shouting a litany of slurs and curses upon Enrico, his parents, and his children that would have made her father proud. I led her away after a few minutes, worried that we would get mugged out here, or worse, that Enrico would be stupid enough to open the door and Liz would kick him in the gonads, resulting in a lawsuit, for sure. We decided to blow off a night in Chicago, and breakfast at the Golden Apple, and drive straight back. It wasn't until New Buffalo that Liz stopped cursing and kicking the dashboard. By Kalamazoo, we had decided to sell our instruments and get married. Not the most romantic of wedding proposal stories, but I'd like to think our profound and unwavering love supercedes the trifles of mere romance. Or something like that.

* * *

Richard's Notebook, page 66

Okay, here's how the ending goes. Junk white face velvet skirt. Flowing. Stop. The beach. No, the moon. No, a dungeon. Click the White House. Naked in the Lincoln Bedroom with Buchanan. It's a joke, son. Get way from me, you bother me, enter. HA HA Mexican hat dance on the '57 Chevy horn. Turquoise or some other sick-o color. Okay, here's the climax. You roll over with sunglasses and a pencil mustache and hold up the palm of your left hand and written in the black marker is the word "Jesus" on the other palm that you hold up slowly and silently. No music here: Lives. You smile and fall back into bed and the camera rises above your and circles out the room, circles the film out and no credits on the white screen and the little boys and girls go home and shoot their mommies and daddies in the brains with laser hunting rifles that Daddy leaves loaded on the kitchen table for hunting those freaking squirrels.

T-shirt—I am my own sequel.

I need to make thirty grand off this book so I can go to Paris for a weekend and still pay off my debt. Fucking student loans. I wish I was a Brit. Tell all your friends to buy this book. But don't tell them how bad you think it sucked. At least it has a cool cover.

Richard posed nude for his roommate during freshman year. His roommate was a boy with bad teeth and straw hair who could not draw. Making everything all Pollack in pencil. Still, boys were naked and not changing in the locker room. I think you know what I am trying to say.

The sun rose slowly above the ocean and filled the sky with yellow, and the waves were my heartbeat. The world lay in my outstretched fever. IT was time to go home. The war was over.

The drama of human experience is inaction.

The camera is shoved so deep into your throat that you can't breathe. The lens is now your esophagus. The lens is very hard, though, and you feel something gurgling and a little confused. The director has you lying on a metal examining table for what is a rather delicate procedure. He is practicing universal precautions. A midget wearing a turban with a fake, red ruby as his third eye enters and speaks.

A day in the life. A life of days. Of days and nights too. We are lost in the night. Among the baby-faced dirt and granite-farced artists examining the universe and finding it existent. Or non. *Claro que sis se existan/ El cielo/ Los nublos y los niños. Se periden. El equipo gano por que no?*

The phone rings.

Black-handled phone filled with germs.

—Sup?

Ju no eet.

Yea, baby.

Yea, Yea baby, yea baby, yea.

—Vid-krell-chuzzah.

Get down on it.

M'fo.

No thanks, I don't believe in cops anymore.

—I'm sure many of them are nice folks.

That movie with the angel that came to earth with Peter Falk in it, *Angels in the Outfield*, I think it was. I read online that it is being remade. I am going to e-mail Stephen and tell him he should audition. He's always gotten along really well with children and monkeys. I think it has an updated plot to reflect our more sophisticated modern sensibility.

The little boy at the birthday party. They all laughed at the poor little angel and his busted angel ass all laying on the poor little angel floor, rolling in the poor little angel sawdust, and I felt like smashing into a cake I did to teach him a lesson. To teach him a lesson, I did. Do you know why? Why, Mama? Because I taught him a lesson.

The plot is the skeleton upon which the humanity hangs.

Exterior.
Small suburban house—a ranch. Brick. And another. Next to another, and they all blend into a mute, dull background as Stephen walks by. It is a brisk October evening and the length of shadow becomes absorbed into the wind and the grass. There are leaves that blow along the sidewalk and swirl and tease.

Stephen is walking and wearing blue jeans and sneakers and a blue-hooded sweatshirt beneath a red, flannel hunting jacket. His hands are deep into the pockets of his coat, but still they are cold. It is unusually cold tonight and the sky hints of early snow, the way the clouds are gray and expansive, luminous in the twilight. Backlit by the moon. He left his hat at home and he thinks to himself how severely he regrets this oversight.

He stops in front of Mickey Felton's house and he sees that Mickey's dad still has not sold the car, some kind of a mid-'80s Dodge sedan. Two years ago, Mrs. Felton took Mickey, who suffered from an underdeveloped ego as well as cerebral palsy, into the car. She sat him, sleeping or medicated, reclined in the back seat. She was in the front seat and left the car running in the garage.

When Mr. Felton came walking home from Tony's Bar after Monday night football, he found them both alive, but barely. By the time the ambulance got there and rushed them over to St. Margaret's on the north side of town (money), they were both basically brain-dead. More or less. It took Mr. Felton not more than fifty-three hours to have the doctors pull the plug(s) on them. They died within seven minutes of each other, the missus at 1:08 P.M. and Mickey at 1:15 P.M.

It was in all the papers. Stephen's mom clipped out the stories and kept them in a red vinyl scrapbook, which she looked at when Stephen was not around. One time, Stephen caught her though. She looked all guilty and weird and Stephen didn't ever say anything about it.

Anyway, the car was still there.

Title Screen: *Ulysses, An American Film with Words*

Characters: Stephen. Tallest of the bunch. A garrulous young man with great warmth and humor and a dark streak that you see in his eyes sometimes. Dark hair these days, pale skin. Irish.

Richard: Slender and vaguely WASPy or like the young Bishop White, although he is descended from Eastern European stock. Hyper smart in that esoteric dead language way-computers. No one knows that he is gay. Shhhh.

Liz: Very short and slender with mutable hair. She teaches Latin to children with terminal illnesses at some local hospice. Or maybe it just seems that way. Dutch.

David: Kicked out of college. Kicked our to medical school too in Puerto Rico for writing his discharge reports in blank verse. Once organized a strike for employees at the Lima Zoo. Lima, Ohio. Short, stocky, and brown straight hair. Eye glasses make him seem wise.

* * *

Liz's Notebook, page 89

There are words that fall staccato.
When we recoil in horror despite rising courage.
The scourge is not our paralysis but enuresis.
Good Stephen. your eyes are so cool and inviting.
Of course the little girlies come lo a-crawling onto your lap.
Waiting for estrogen hallucination.

Low on their bellies, golden boughs or soft backs
Your eyes are stars that shine despite you.
But when you cast away the callow, true vision.
You must accept what the gods condone—your contusion.
Recall, Jimmy too was blinded by light, and all blind by shade
'cept those borne not of woman solely, nor lonely women made.

I love you, Stephen, but I am not going to go through with this. I am going insane. I have not written a new song in a year. I am going to have a baby. I am not an artist. There, I said it. I am not an artist and neither is David and neither is Richard. You might be. You just might be, you have the stomach for it. We don't. We are just people. Please forgive us.

* * *

T-Shirt Promo Movie Slogans

Life is based on truth.
You are a freak.
I am a freak.
Truth is for winners!
Stately, plump.
Jimmy.
Fascism is fun.
Sell your brain.
Ford's in his flyvver (and all's right in the world).
Where is my cat, Matt?
I would rather be a mule.
Ulysses, Live on Tour. With words.
I killed my father, what did you do today?
Jubilate Deo.
Gregory sure was great.
Epictetus kicks ass.

My parents went to the seventh circle of hell and all I got was this lousy T-shirt.

* * *

An Electronic Mail message from Stephen

The ending of it your gonna love it if you're a po—mo super fly. Face into the camera. White cake face like a mime. I stare at the camera and say, "I guess I'm a movie that can't be made. What kind of way is that to end anything?" The days are long and I give sort of a half grin kind of smirk deal all vapid and con man super shy boy and then I'll close my eyes for six seconds and open them up and say, "All mimes are heroes even you and me. The strings come in full swell Sibelius, the Finn, scraper of men, and then the white the white the white and no credits fuck the union this is my fucking movie that not going to get made. I can not have any freaking credits if I want to. Who cares if no one sees it? Either I know it or I don't either way it don't save the city on the hill if you know what I mean.

Then all the boys and girls go home and watch reruns of something on the television. Except the one kid who snuck into the film who's only fourteen and he goes home gets out a notebook and he writes a poem ode to a mime. Except the rhyme scheme but his mime dream is enough to forgive him for it is so innocent is it. Mimes even onto original to Athens but the boy does not know any better he hungers for the mom. The mime poet of it all. For the mime of the poet of it all. We are saved for another day.

Call me.

The Scene. Richard. David.

Richard pretends to like the music. The rock and roll isn't for me. The blaring. The monks of St. Francis. The goodly friars. Their beards all in a row.

It was 4:00 A.M. The newspapers were spread on the floor. The light was on in the noisy living room across the street. The air was still. Still, I awoke to say that it was really just the air of vagueness that drew me to it initially.

He returned from the Midwest quite fundamentally

unchanged, but our circumstances had, and there was little that we now agreed on. My life had passed in my bedroom in my basement studio. Most people consider that my period of withdrawal. I understand it to be my time of great awakening. In the confines of my studio at 4:00 A.M., guilt writing the necessary reading, etc. that took over me, and in my brain, the insight that I, too, must fail. Just as others far greater had failed before me. It was no epiphany really, but a subtle shift of perception.

On one recent occasion, at a New Year's Eve Party, an old acquaintance of mine handed me a small, clear, plastic sandwich bag filled with photographs that were cut into small pieces. The photographs were of his genitalia. He claimed it to have invented the next wave of cinema. I smiled supportively as that is my disposition, but thought to myself that I hoped the *Seinfeld* rerun was not a good one, because I'd really much rather be home watching reruns than being here.

Later that morning, though, I'd mellowed a bit. Perhaps his relentless enthusiasm for the 95 Theses, or whatever that Swedish filmmaking "school" calls themselves, wore me down. But I lay in bed, tucked next to Liz, my legs draped across hers, enjoying the sense of her skin on mine. I could feel her warm breath on my chest. I stroked her long brown hair and prayed we die like this someday, fifty years from now. And I thought of the snow that falls despite my green candle perched on the sill, painted white. The winter sky is white, as is the moon. Heaven is white. The sheets on the bed, too, are white. And crisp. The shadows dance on the wall, cast from green candle. Light. That is the new cinema, I should have told him. Feeling excited and bloodied now. The new cinema is the word. The image is dead. Our eyes are blinded. I drifted off to sleep, content.

I fought Richard once at Cape Hatteras, and I would fight him again.

The debate: Free Will.
                       All I'll say is I free-willed his sorry ass downtown. But now, he has destroyed the lineage of some such thing.

R: It's just a question of when you believe life begins.
Me: What do you mean?
R: I mean that what all this bullshit comes down to. All the debating and crying and biting about the film and holding forth about how boring our lives are and how we aren't wearing this or that, and being in bed by eleven because we have to be to work at eight in our little fucking cubes. Having to fill out requisition slips for pens and staples. Flirting with the copy girls or boys, or whoever it is we flirt with to remind us that we aren't in the sixth ring of hell. So why not kill him?
Me: It's illegal.
R: My friend, you know there are laws, and there is truth.
Me: Save it for your memoir.
R: Borne of distilled Existentialism 101. I don't know why we're even having this conversation. You don't have the balls to kill anyone. You didn't even kiss a girl until you were seventeen. Looks away. I always thought you might be, well, you know, gay.
Me: What can I say?
R: Nothing. Kiss me, you fool.

They kiss and fade out.

* * *

David, On Camera

"Liz's sister is a lesbian. There, I've said it. If her parents ever read this book, they are going to kill me. But she should not hide any longer. I am outing her because I love her. She needs to be free. We must all be free. On the count of three, let's all take off our masks and be free, shall we? Let's all breathe deep and repeat after me. I am beauty, I am super, I am free. Louder, everybody now. Can you hear me with your special ears? Are you listening to the words I am not saying aloud? Then you too must be free. Indeed!"

* * *

Richard's Notebook, page 111

Okay, here's how the ending goes: Junk white face velvet skirt. Flowing. Stop. The beach. No, the moon. No, a dungeon. Click. The white house. Naked in the Lincoln Bedroom. With Buchanan. It's a joke, son, get away from me, boy, you bother me. Enter. Ha Ha. Mexican hat dance on the '57 Chevy horn, turquoise, or some other sick-o color. Okay, here's the climax. You roll over with sunglasses and a pencil mustache and hold up the palm of your left hand and written in black marker is the word "Jesus," and on the other palm, you hold up slowly, silently, no music here, Christ. You smile and fall back into bed and the camera rises above you and circles out the room. Circles the film out and no credits on the white screen, and the little boys and the little girls go home and shoot their mommies and daddies in the brains with laser hunting rifles that Daddy leaves loaded on the kitchen table for hunting those fucking squirrels.

Aren't you sick of this shit/shtick yet?

Richard on Camera, Medium Close-up

"I think it was Joyce or somebody who said that in actuality, killing is just a byproduct of simple cognitive reframing. Just a subtle shift in attitude, in perception. Killing is not evil. Notions of evil that it is some absolute, some thing, some entity, are almost laughably uptight—very Midwestern. There is a continuum of evil but it does not bear the obvious marks, the obvious indications. It is almost imperceptible, really. Perhaps, the linkage is from Nietzche to Joyce to Hitler to Bandura, not through Freud, as I suggested earlier. Just a subtle shift of perception."

Then, music, as if coming from a Victrola, a melancholy tune circa 1933, with accordion and female vocals in French.

Liz to the camera, "I can't believe Richard's bizarre theories are going to be in the movie. Is Stephen nuts? I think he has lost his mind. I mean, he had something so tender and simple, and now he's getting all muddled. Maybe this is just one of those elaborate jokes Stephen and Richard are always trying to pull off. They get so Leopold and Loeb sometimes. Kinda creepy. I'm really thinking about dropping out of this. It's just too . . . I don't know . . . it's just wrong . . . Richard, you never can tell, eyes were averted though. I think he was bluffing.

Stephen, looking tan and fit, on the beach in Los Angeles, "We all deserve fame in our own sexy videos.

It's just a subtle shift. That's all it is."

* * *

I got home from night school at about 10:30 P.M., dead from a full day of work and driving thirty miles each way up to Beech Hills. Liz had a small dinner of tomato soup and a cheese sandwich waiting for me on the dining room table. There was a candle lit and Miles Davis' *Kind of Blue* was filling the chilly room. We exchanged pleasantries and she told me about one of the crazy kids in her classes who punched her in the belly and called her a whore. I was incensed, but she just laughed it off. "He's got problems, you know, ugly divorce, never sees Dad, living with Grandma, that sort of thing. What does Barzun recommend we do with those sorts of kids?" I said I didn't know, but I know I'd like to do something to him. She said that she had gotten a call from Richard and he sounded kind of down in the dumps. Stephen isn't returning his calls, and he's thinking about getting a job with the government. He's thinking about dropping out of the movie. We looked at each other. I knew that Liz had been thinking about the same thing. Just being tired and fed up with all of it, and it not really seeming to be going anywhere.

"He was going on and on about all kinds of stuff in that Richard sort of way. I told him to call back and leave it on the voice mail so you could hear it. Are you ready?"

"Is anyone ever ready for Richard when he's on a roll? If I listen to it, am I going to have bad dreams?"

"Probably, but give it a try anyway."

I picked up the phone and dialed the numbers she told me, as I never can remember all the codes and passwords that rule my existence. Here is the message Richard left:

"Hey guys, Richard here, this whole movie thing is going nowhere. NOWHERE. FAST. We should just forget about it. Let Stephen do it if he wants to, but I'm done with it. You guys should drop it too, get on with your lives already. Just get some guts and move to Paris. Forget the mothers and fathers and the fantasies of the bare belly kiss. Forget about the Hollywood genocide and the dirtcore fratricide. Forget about the finger painting and the moon and the thing itself. Forget about silence and the silence that is not silence, but that is words. And that you never gave me my Thomas Wolfe back. That's okay, books should never be reread when you're alive. Forget about these things and move there, like he would if he didn't have to kill his father and all. Okay, that's it. I'll talk to you guys later."

I stood there for a minute. I didn't know what to think, let alone what to say. My initial reaction was to roll my eyes at Richard's rants, as I usually did. This time, there was a sound in his voice that resonated with me. It was less pedantic than usual, somehow more tired, almost vulnerable. I hadn't heard him sound that way in a long while and I think it summed up how we were all starting to feel—just tired and beaten down. We couldn't agree on anything. We had no money, Stephen was getting more and more Hollywood, with Mr. Black's "connections" and all that, lots of parties but no cash. Our initial dreams of creating something worthwhile and interesting seemed to be getting farther and farther away. And we were all getting tired of the film, art, and each other. Still, I wasn't ready to let go. Even though he was hiding it pretty well in his L.A. glamour love, I knew Stephen wanted this to be beautiful. More importantly, a document that Colin Darden did exist on this planet, and that beneath the ink-stained fingers and nicotine-stained teeth beats the heart of a true poet—a lover of words, glorious and filthy words. Without getting all *Hoosiers* on you, I believed that has to count for something.

Jordan's on the pine needles. He needs help. I'm with you.

I know they're going to catch me. Sitting at my desk idly. Starting at the memoranda on the wall. Making lists in my notebooks. Lists about books to buy, books to read, projects to develop, favorite words, favorite restaurants, favorite colors, least favorite politicians. Jotting notes in my notebook. Chatting with my cubicle neighbors. Gossiping about our bosses, complaining about how much work we have to do. I know they're going to catch and fire me. I will have my car and house repossessed. They'll throw me in debtor's prison and I'll sweep pigeon shit from beneath the railroad underpass. Perhaps, this will be for the best, my current disposition being what it is. The black mood and all. Snapping at Liz for being without direction, only because I am without direction. My ears are open but I do not hear.

I took an extra ten minutes for lunch today because my boss was not here and I do not feel guilty about it. I was at the bookstore, thumbing though books I don't have the cash to buy. Books the library does not carry. *ABC of Reading*. The new Saul Bellow novella. Porta, Zweig, and Morrow. Their words flow over me like the warm, soft spray of ocean water, leaving me with a thin coat of brine and sand in my hair. I wonder why Stephen does not talk about books anymore. His immense vocabulary and innate ability to see through the morass of theory and chicanery, to see the real, amazes and humbles me. He can see things in a way that I can not, despite my pretensions. A gift from his father, for sure. Why is he throwing it all away? Why doesn't he think he is throwing it all away? This stupid movie. The more I talk to people about it, the more I wonder if as many people love James Joyce as I thought they did. Did you hear that new theory that James Joyce did not write *Ulysses* by himself?

That Sylvia Beech actually rewrote massive portions of it herself, but Joyce couldn't tell because of his vision problems? He was about to have her murdered by some Italian thugs that Pound knew when all the critical acclaim started rolling in. He was in a bind because he couldn't come out and say he didn't write this incredible book, especially since he knew her revisions vastly improved his book. Apparently, his initial structure was to follow just one character, Buck Mulligan, over three days, not three characters over one day. I read it on *www.myacademy.com*. You can read it for yourself to see whether you are convinced.

I'm thinking about buying a video camera myself to keep in my car so I can film scenes for the movie at lunchtime. It will be about me. It will show me doing everything I ordinarily do at lunchtime. It will be without speaking. People do not like movies with speaking anymore. The chitter-chatter is a burden sent to bog down the excitement of the fisticuffs that defy gravity and the sex.

For example,

David looks at his watch. We are all looking at his watch. But there are no numbers or hands on the watch's face. She's probably not home so he picks up the paper. Front page of the *Metro* section. Seventy-two-year-old lady crashes though the patio door of her neighbor's condo, killing her neighbor's springer spaniel. She was pulled from the car by her eighty-two-year-old neighbor and severely beaten with a dictionary as several neighbors looked on. The driver was returning home from the Westville Secretary of State office, having failed her vision test due to being legally blind. She got her license though, as her physician wrote a note saying she was going in for surgery in about six months or so. True story.

Editor's Note: In Michigan we call the place where you get your driver's license, get new license plates and other car stuff, the Secretary of State's office, not the Department of Motor Vehicles

(DMV). I am sure there is a reason for this, but as I failed *Michigan History: The Great Lakes are Great Friends* class, I am at a loss as to what it is. Sorry for the confusion about this.

Stephen in Chicago

He was sitting alone in his dark apartment, watching a rough edit of "JJ's Eyes" when he heard a knock on the door. He turned sharply. Startled, he crossed the tiled floor in his bare feet. His heart rate was elevated and he was breathing rapidly. Who the hell could it be now at this time of night? What time is it anyway? Three o'clock—not in the morning, I'm sure.

"Just a second," he said as he fumbled with the lock. Fucking idiot landlord, he thought, pushing and twisting the rusted bracket. He finally got it opened. It was a boy. Fifteen maybe. Well groomed. Tallish. Tall as he. Thinner, perhaps. Still. Red hair. Cut as is the style. Green army pants and black sweater. If Stephen were in front of a mirror, he would be standing in front of himself ten (fourteen) years earlier.

"Hi, my name is Joseph McCartney, I'm selling magazine subscriptions to raise money for the St. Francis High School football team. We're trying to buy new uniforms."

"Did you say McCarthy?"

"No, McCartney."

"Irish?"

"On my father's side. My mother's Jewish."

"Jimmy wouldn't like that, would he, Joey?"

"Joseph. Jimmy who?"

"Oh, James Joyce."

"Who?"

"James Joyce. The novelist. The Irish novelist."

"Did he write that one about heroin which they made into that movie?"

"Did you enjoy it?"

"Yes, the guy going in the toilet was awesome."

"Right. Well, you should check out *Ulysses,* it's even better."

"So did you want to buy any?"

"What were you selling again? I wasn't paying attention."

"I'm selling magazines for the St. Francis High School football team. Would you like to help us out?"

"Sorry, kid, I'm a soccer player at heart."

"Well, it's not to late to repent, sir."

With that, Stephen was compelled to invite him in and purchase magazines.

Stephen and Joseph, or Joey, as Stephen called him, bantered for a good ten minutes about college plans, the Roman Catholic high school experience, the vagaries of magazine salesmanship, Pope Gregory the Great, and the new Sheeler exhibition downtown. Joseph's mother was an assistant curator at the MCIA. Stephen hated de Sheeler but did a report on him for eleventh-grade English. He got a B+ on the paper—his lowest grade that year. He got a 5 on the AP English exam and minored in English at Waterloo College, ultimately being dismissed from a Harvard doctoral program in literature. Why he was telling this to this stranger, a high school boy nonetheless, he was not sure.

Stephen bought some liberal pro-labor propaganda sheet. All "eco-conscious" on recycled paper, with poor graphics to prove some point.

"If you don't mind me asking, what is that you're watching?"

"Oh that, I forgot I still had it on. It's a movie, I guess. Some friends and I are working on it."

"Looks like a cross between early Goon Squad and Pi," Joseph said.

"What did you say? What does a young whipper-snapper like you know about that sort of thing? That is exactly what I'm going for. By the way, do you think this scene here, the musical montage, what do you think? Tell me, be honest now . . ."

Joseph stared intently at the phantasmagoric scene of James Joyce (Stephen) riding a motor scooter through the rainy Parisian streets, being chased by a mob of teenage girls, only to lose control and slide into the carts of books in front of Shakespeare and Co. Joyce stands up and is confronted by an angry looking Gertrude

Stein (Liz) who pulls off his eyepatch. She smacks him across the face, then plants a soul kiss on his pasty white lips. The music sounds like a deep trance version of *Singing in the Rain*.

"Well, it's not bad, I guess . . . I mean . . . I probably don't get what you were going for . . ."

"What do you think? Don't hold back, Joseph."

"It is a bit silly, don't you think?"

"Silly? Yes, of course, it's silly. But is it bad silly, or good silly? That's what I need to know."

"Not funny silly, if that's what you mean."

Stephen looked away from Joseph towards the television set. He picked up the remote control and pressed stop.

"Yes, I think you're absolutely right. I think it really is bad silly."

"Hey, don't listen to me, Mr. Darden, I'm just a high school kid. What do I know? Why don't you show it to my dad—he would know. He's sort of in the film business."

"Oh really, who's your dad?"

"Omar Black, he's an agent . . ."

"I know who he is . . . he's one of the most important agents in Chicago . . . He was instrumental in getting that kid who played "Long Duck Dong" in *Sixteen Candles*. Didn't he almost single-handedly get Chris Farley into Second City? Wow, he's your father? I thought your last name was McCartney? Divorce."

"Black is a pseudonym. Changed it when he moved to Chicago in the late '70s. Apparently there was a lot of anti-Irish sentiment when he first got here. Don't forget, the Shamrock riots of 1978 were still in everyone's mind. So, he wanted a fresh start. Da always believed that the Irish were about as oppressed as African-Americans in this country, so he changed his working name to Black."

"Can you believe that people could be so mean to one another?" Stephen mused.

"Of course, but not to the Irish," Joseph replied with a twinkle in his green eyes.

"You little leprechaun, you. You might actually lead me to the pot of gold at the end of the rainbow."

"Stick with me, sir, I'll make sure you find the pot of gold at both ends of the rainbow! Of course, I'll want a finder's fee, and judging by the film, I'll take that in cash."

With that, Stephen and Joseph laughed uproariously, grabbed each other by the arm and danced an authentic Irish jig. After they had danced and drank Irish whiskey, Joseph took leave of his new discovery. Stephen watched Joseph walk down the street from the side window. He smiled, watching the kid eagerly but coolly walk to some great, uncertain future.

David's Bad Dreams

A long time before Liz died, her husband had recurring fantasies, well, not exactly flashes, more of images of Liz and Richard in bed in the act of intercourse. Several times a day, this picture would flash into his consciousness. Day or night. Reading Oppen. Praying. Running. Accompanied by the requisite core of rage. At whom? Richard, for his betrayal? At Liz, for her dying? At his mother for abandoning him as a young boy to go play tennis with the neighbor lady? Perhaps, too, there is a generous basin for self-loathing. Thank god they did not have children yet. Now, maybe society can spend its money on something useful, for Christ's sake.

David and Liz on the town.

We sit at the sandwich place across from the bookstore in West Village. Liz and I are watching the auto parade down Michigan Avenue. The stores, as you know, have no street side entrances. All free-floating humans and humanoids are banned from using the sidewalk. Who can blame the city when the cars bust through at 55mph? Would you like to be pushing a baby stroller three inches away from these autos? I wrote a letter to a city councilman requesting either build underground walkways or give us jetpacks. Who is brave enough to cross the street these days?

We enter the shops, the bookstore, and the restaurant from the rear. (Please do not read any psychosexual bullshit into the previous line when you are writing your dissertations and preparing questions for interviewing me for the cover of *Time* and *Sports Illustrated*.) So this must be the front when you actually consider it. Regardless, it's the only way in. We were feeling giddy so we walked. We carry walkie-talkies to hear each other talking above the racing motors and wind shift of the autos. We cross Garretson, a quiet street. Then proceed through approximately six acres of parking lot. Ten billion autos right here. No sidewalk. Each year, about two or three thousand people are smooshed by the beautiful gilded autos zipping through. One lady's estate got sued for causing emotional damages to the driver after getting run over by her car. The driver won six billion dollars. I had the chance to run someone over once, but I figured it would be our local hockey god and I would be chased down and clubbed like a mongrel seal.

Liz's eating hamburgers and I'm nibbling on pita and Ritalin, waiting for the goddamn mjadra. It is so amazingly goodly herely. Liz starts making a scene about her having a tumor and how this might be her last meal. It just sort of upsets my stomach. I have to take most of my mjadra as carryout. I'll eat it after she goes to bed.

The scene, the screening room.

White stucco walls. Three on the chair, Stephen standing.
Low monotone keyboard. Constant buzz. At the base of your neck.
Low feeling of lowness.
The silver screen was blank.
Stephen crosses the room and turns on the projector as if in slow motion. Agonizingly slow. The light floats at the lenses and splashes out at the screen and we see every wave and we see every packet. Every one splashing onto the silver screen.
The camera pans the room on to each of the faces of the three.

Liz, lower lip bit. Red lipstick.
Richard, no affect.
David, mouth opened slightly, eyes piercing. Brow furrowed.
Stephen, fingers on his cheek. Hand on other elbow. Staring intently.

The scene floats on for an eternity. The camera stopped. Fixes on the screen and it is a scene of four people sitting in a white stucco room, watching a film. There is a low, buzzing drone.

The repetition and the droning calms us. In the space of the stillness and in the noise, we can open a new heart in our chests. One with eyes and intuition.

The click of the projector underneath the low, soft drone of the projector buzzing in our head. Warms our brains and our necks and our shoulders. In the space and in the noise, the world falls, but it is not blackness. We are connected to a larger world, a world of greatness and goodness. The world inside our secret.

The camera pans across a painting.

There are six lines on black canvas @ 10001.

Voice Over (Richard): Six lines confine us. Without form, without borders. Defined. Ah, beauty of Ulysses paradox. Sweet, sweet sweat. We speak our thoughts, but they are unexamined. They are examined but invisible. We are thought to be lost. The primacy. The head. And such a petulant smirk. All ghetto hair, negro. Stomach acid burns. It is the effect of art, my friend. It is the effect which art has upon us. Do not be afraid, you will not die. Not even art can do that. Or can it?

Another phone call from Richard

Richard called at 1:00 A.M. last night/this morning to talk to me for a new idea for a film he has. A little girl is sued as a drug courier. Her dad is blown away before our eyes. Her mother od'd. The girl goes on a spiritual journey. Ends up being taken in by a blind rabbi, who teaches her Hebrew. The climax is a scene when he goes on and on about Mt. Moriah and events that transpire there. It's a tripped-out scene and it ends with the rabbi holding a large knife over the prostrate girl, with a tight shot of her face. And she is essential angelic beauty and grace, her face still, as if she was simply waiting to fall asleep. *Moonlight Sonata*, muted and barely audible. The calm cannot be described here adequately, nor in Richard's telling. But I know the look he spoke about. I have never seen it, only imagined it. Kneeling in the front pew at St. Mary's. The altar rising before me. The crucifix rising before me. Jesus rising before me. I am unafraid for once in my anxious life and I am longing for the Eucharist to fill me. The communion. I know the look, but like I said, it's from imagination.

Still, I told him he should get his head back in the game and spend his energy working on our film, for God's sake. The script's still a shambles and we have no fucking money yet. The production system is being altered beyond recognition. We may be on the wrong side of history on this one. It seems that people may not be interested in a documentary about Joyce's vision difficulties, and the writing of *Ulysses* may not be the cash bonanza we initially thought. Our early projections were too optimistic. Too bright-eyed. Too bleary-eyed. But the early polling seemed so promising. We were going to have Matlock represent the book in the pornography hearings.

Richard: This project is going nowhere.
David: We just need one break. Just one. We'll be set.
Richard: I might bail out of this. I just feel we're spinning our wheels. Where it's just a mishmash. And I think we're doing it for all the wrong reasons.
David: I agree. But we still need to do it. It's bigger than our petty squabbles.
Richard: That's not what I mean. We're doing this to be rich when we should be doing it to be famous. If you get famous, the rest will follow.
David: If you're rich, then who cares about fame?
Richard: Then play the lottery and don't waste my time with this goddamn film thing.

David: I do play the lottery. Every single day. When I hit big, you're going to be crawling over here on your slimy little belly, begging at my shoes for a few bucks. I may have pity on you and drop a quarter into your quivering, outstretched hand. I may not. I may simply say a prayer for you and walk away. I don't know. We'll have to wait and see.

Richard: You're such a freak. The only reason you put yourself out there is to be consumed. To have people know you. Know who you are as you walk down the street, or slide into the booth at the Denny's. Just loving that people are turning their heads and saying, "Isn't that so and so, that one guy?" And you are loving it. You love every single minute of it. You complain about it and you talk about the burdens of your fans, of your public. You talk of your agent and your lawyer. And how the whole scene is tired and ruining your artistic abilities. How you just need to get away from it all for a few days, a few weeks. Maybe go to a spa, go on a cruise. Just get out of this town because the people are eating you alive. But you start realizing you can't, you can't go. You just can't leave it. You are afraid if you leave, they will not let you come back, and then where would you be? Just where you are now and that scares the shit out of you.

David: I'm tired, Richard. I really am. I'm just really goddamned tired.

Richard: You're depressed. You're angry at yourself for sticking around this God-awful city, just watching people die. You want to get away so people can realize what a true genius you are, but you know you'll have to leave Ireland to do that. Only then will the leeches and the morons see you for who you are. The savior of the English language.

David: What are we talking about? This is just driving me nuts. Do real people talk like this? What do real people say to each other? I mean, God! I just want to talk about the baseball game or something. Can't we just do that? Talk about the Tigers beating the Orioles last night. Wasn't that a perfect night at the ball park? The gentle breeze coming in from right center field. The fierce pitching. The tenacious base running.

Richard: Do animal rights activists want sports teams to change their names?
David: I need to go to bed and die now.
Richard: Good night.
David: All right. I'll see you tomorrow.
Richard: Not if I see you first.
David: What does that mean? I never really understood what that means. Does it mean you're going to kill me or something if you see me? Should I be wary of you skulking about in the shadows? What does it mean?
Richard: Good night, sweet David.

As I drift off to sleep, I've not given up hope yet. I mean this book, this man, his soul, is such an important part of our national consciousness. Who can forget when they received their first copy of *Ulysses*? Or when a Joyce impersonator came to my tenth birthday party Come on now. Or the television commercial where Joyce was boxing against Jack Dempsey, and they hug each other and crack open a frosted malt liquor beverage? Maybe the problem is over-saturation. I still think the scene where Beech is chasing him through the Left Bank on those motorcycles would be hair-raising. Or the dinner party where Joyce first met Proust. Apparently, words were passed and the evening ended in any ugly brawl, with Joyce having his glasses broken. They say that Proust was under the influence of Prozac at the time and couldn't be blamed for what he said. About Joyce being a secret agent and all. There's no denying though that the *Joyce Variety Show*, sponsored by the Fjord Motor Company, was responsible for inventing World War II. I've seen the proof.

Neil, the staff historian.

Then there was the bizarre information that I discovered when discussing the project with Neil, an affable staff historian, who was employed at the Elkville Historical Museum. He looks exactly like someone who would be employed at the Elkville Historical

Museum, so I won't bother describing him to you. I was wandering in the basement, looking at the dioramas, taking notes for the film, when he sauntered down and stood behind me. We stood in silence for several minutes before he started talking.

"Beautiful exhibit, isn't it?"

"Yes. Quite amazing."

"The Potawanamee lived in this area for hundreds of years before the French settlers pushed them out. Camped right here near the Rouge River."

"Well, you could do that sort of thing before the Nazi started dumping shit in it."

I knew I shouldn't have said that, but it was too late. I felt my face flush with embarrassment.

He cleared his throat and said, "You know, I might have something you'd be interested in."

He looked over his shoulder to make sure no one was around, then led me through a wooden door with two dead bolts on it. Stenciled on the door with blue spray paint were the following, "Hazardous Materials, Keep Out." I was certain this is how I would meet my demise. He was an undercover Fjord Cop and he was going to take me to the soundproof back room and put a bullet in my temple. We walked down a long, narrow corridor that was gray with exposed pipes and pumps, lit by a string of bare light bulbs down the center of the hall. The clickety-click of his heels, a reverberating percussion in my head. Clickety-click, clickety-click. My hands were sweating and my throat was narrowing. I thought about doing a Bruce Lee on the back of his head, but knew I would look ridiculous, so I passed. He led me in through a metal doorway that was locked with several locks and a sign that said, "Authorized Personnel Only." I began praying the rosary under my breath and thanked God that I was wearing underwear.

We entered a room that I immediately recognized as some sort of research library annex. This would be a familiar place to die, and I often hoped to die when in such a place, especially reading some psychology journal, so I began feeling less apprehensive. The walls were lined with bookshelves and books bound in a variety of materials—cloth, leather, and even many black, three-ring binders. There was a large oak table, with a Tiffany style lamp bathing the room in a warm, soft glow. He motioned me to have a seat at one of two leather, padded desk chairs seated on opposite sides of the table. I slid into the chair and began scanning the walls. From what I could tell, they appeared to be the entire catalogs of several mid-twentieth century publishing houses. I could see Beckett, Anna Freud, Gide, Hemingway. I was certain that there must be some Joyce in there, but I did not see it before Neil returned from one of the shelves, seated himself across from me and slid a single manila folder towards me. I stood looking at it for a moment, deeply ambivalent, as I always was during novel experiences.

"Open it," he said, "it's okay."

I pulled it closer to me, picked it up and opened it like I was reading a book. A single sheet of paper slid to the ground. Neil sighed and made a weird, throaty, whistling sound as I bent over to pick it up. I apologized, realizing that whatever this was, it was awfully important to him. Probably a fucking dry cleaning invoice from Mr. Fjord, I thought to myself.

It was not a dry cleaning invoice, I realized upon closer inspection, but a typewritten letter written on the letterhead of "McCormick, Finney, and O'Halloran, ESQ, Counsellors and Barristers of Law, '87 Trinity Street, Dublin, Ireland." It was dated July 17, 1942 and read as follows:

> *Dear Mr. Fjord,*
>
> *Thank you so much for your recent inquiry into the acquisition of the "personal items" of the late Mr. James Joyce for the new Museum of Americana that you are establishing in the United States.*
>
> *We regret to inform you that the executors of Mr. Joyce's estate do not wish to part with these "items" at this time. As you know, the death of Mr. Joyce and the*

horrific war that is currently transpiring has had a significant emotional impact on the family of Mr. Joyce, and the family does not feel that allowing these items to leave Dublin is prudent at this time.

I assure you that your generous purchase offer in the sum of well over a quarter of a million dollars was greatly appreciated by the family. It was of some condolence to them that the works of Mr. Joyce have had such a personal impact on you so that you are willing to create an entire wing of the museum to the life and work of Mr. Joyce, especially celebrating the impact his work has had on the American culture. Hopefully, the original notebooks, manuscripts, and novel that Mr. Joyce was working on at the time of his death—An American Film—will still provide ample resources for the development of this portion of your museum.

Please feel free to contact us if we can be of any help in facilitating this exciting intellectual endeavor.

Respectfully,
Simon O'Halloran
Attorney-at-Law

I read it several times, convinced that I was looking at some hoax, a ruse, a con.

"It's the real deal," Neil said, "the real deal."

"Are you sure, I mean . . . are you sure?"

"Oh yes, we've had it authenticated and corroborated and carbon-fourteen'd. It's the real fucking deal."

This convinced me, as Neil did not seem to be the type to use the word "fucking" or any permutation thereof in a glib or nonchalant manner. He seemed to be a serious fucker. I sat for a moment in a state of shock. It all was beginning to make sense. All the loose threads seemed to be finally coming together. There was still something that was not quite clear yet, something still blurry, forms in the shadows of twilight whose outlines I could not quite discern.

"Neil, what was the initial request for these personal items that the Fjord folks wanted?"

Neil looked a bit nervous. His eyes darted around the room, stopping for a moment at a small red book on a lower shelf. He handed it to me and told me to start banging on the table with it. As I did, Neil began coughing loudly and wrote on a sheet of notebook paper the following words, which I was sworn to obliterate from my memory upon fear of death:

"JJ's Eyes."

I started to ask questions, but Neil quickly covered my mouth. He said that we had been here long enough and were sure to arouse suspicions. I asked him from who, but he didn't answer. Instead, he led me not through the labyrinth as before, but through another staircase that exited to an alley behind the museum. I turned to speak to him, but he slammed the rusty iron door shut. As I reached for the handle to open it, I was stumped—no handle. I thought about pounding on the iron door, but the memory of Neil's white face and beads of nervous perspiration forming on his lips and eyebrow was enough to dissuade me from that action. I raced home to tell Liz about my strange day at the historical museum, only to discover an empty house. Damn, it's Tuesday, she's at her prenatal yoga class. I made a dinner of macaroni and cheese and turned on the news. It was the usual barrage of car crashes, missing foster children, actors holding their children upside down off rollercoaster rides, etc. My ears perked up when the local "News for U" crew broke in at the scene of what appeared to be a massive explosion. I didn't need to hear the blathering announcer say it. I recognized the building, or what remained of it. It was the Elkville Historical Museum. I almost threw up when the man said, "Not believed to be any survivors," thinking about how I almost was blown up. I turned off the television and poured myself a double diet cola. Before I guzzled it, I said a prayer for Neil and for not being blown up myself. The cola tasted especially refreshing.

Liz was astonished to hear my tale when she got home. It sounded so preposterous. I thought so myself. We were both at a loss as to what exactly "JJ's Eyes" had to do with this, but were certain it was involved.

I couldn't fall asleep right away; my mind was a jumble, trying to piece this all together. Liz rubbed my shoulders and sang a song. A hushed lullaby. Sweet. Pure. Innocent. I wanted to disappear into her voice. Her purity. Her gracious gift from God. To lose Richard and the world and to know the peace in her voice. I fell asleep gently and had unusually amusing dreams throughout the night. I can't tell her because dream retelling is just so much tedium anyways. Can't ever get the mood right in words. I only woke up once to use the bathroom. I feel like I'm sleeping better without Valium.

Well, you've convinced me. I will tell you one of my dreams. But it's only because I feel a sense of duty in my efforts to repeat my experiences as honestly and directly as possible. That is, after all, my primary responsibility as an artist. To hell with fame. To hell with money. I have a good-paying job to support me. To free me to be true to my art.

So, anyway, this dream. You're seeing all this through my eyes sometimes. I don't think I ever wear glasses in my dreams. But this is not seem to be affecting my myopia. Into this library where I'm sitting comes Liz. Except it does not look like Liz, it looks like Eleanor Roosevelt. She's really come on to me hard in an amorous way. We walk into a field of daisies and there's a man in a bear suit who comes out from behind a tree and tries to sell me a cheap reproduction of the Magna Carta. I, of course, refuse because in my dream, I already own a copy. The bear is getting all pushy and Liz, who looks like Lil' Orphan Annie, stops the bear with a Glock and the bear explodes and we all get covered with cheez whiz.

Then we go to a mall and play the videogame Street Annihilation. She kicks ass there as well. Then I wake up to go pee. I don't remember after that dream when I wake up, so I wonder if I'm just making it up now to amuse myself. Anyway, the next morning I drive by the historical museum and it is still smoldering. I take Michigan Avenue to work to avoid being followed. I drive for blocks and blocks and see no other living creature. The store fronts have rusted iron bars over broken glass windows. The viaducts are scrawled with spray painted messages in Spanish and English. They are written in a deep code that I can not break. I wonder if the Fjord spies can read them?

At work that day, like most days, I am like a ghost or a spy. I walk from the men's room to my cubicle, keeping them always in the corner of my eye. I refuse to think that I am one of them. They don't recognize me for the great artist that I am. To them, I am a grunt social worker, a man to boot so I get a lot of notice that way. Well, I did at first. But since I successfully managed to go thirty-seven straight weeks without talking to anyone, I'm pretty much left alone. I started this career seven years ago, when a college adviser had me a flip a coin and choose between English and psychology. English lost, so here I am. Which is fine, because the last thing I ever wanted was to corrupt my brilliance with the lure of easy money by running writing workshops or some shit. Some whitebread fraud. All volume and nothing to say. I guess that if I identify so greatly with Joyce, we will stand together as the best pure writers of the twentieth and twenty-first centuries. Anyway, my paperwork is piling up—I have to go now, Bye-bye!

Flash to David driving his car. Bass and drums pounding so loud your ears hurt.

Flash of Stephen brushing his teeth, frothing at the mouth.

Flash of Liz eating an apple.

Flash of David sitting around, looking at a cereal box with James Joyce on the front cover.

Flash, see keyword *Ulysses*. Find.

Stephen's Journal, pages 17-21

A postmodern journal suggested that Telemachos was having an affair with his father. The battle scenes are really just sexual imagery and describe the exquisite sublimation of their love. You know, the bows and arrows and such. Get it? Of course. Makes me sick. That is why I was kicked out of graduate school. I was not one of them. Their words were to deny. They were thumbscrews and cat o' nine tails. How do I explain this perpetual state of alienation to my best friends, to my lovers, to my family? I am never at home, especially when I am home. That is why I clutter my life with details and obsessions, lists and projects, half-finished poems, essays—I am like David in this way; but he is cursed with a spirit that makes him want to help people. What a curious ailment. He shall never be a great writer because of this.

David talks about the people he works with, people whose disabilities, mental retardation, usually, is so severe that they have no ability to make choices. Their mode of existence has been that of the institution where all decisions are made for you. There is a growing body of literature he says to suggest that choice-making ability can be taught, even to severely retarded individuals. One wonders though, that if an individual who has never made a choice is confronted with two items that one likes, then what happens if the individual chooses both? If the selection was one where both options are equally desirable, then what choice is that? If it was between two objects which are both undesirable, then what sort of choice is that? And what reinforcement do you give when they choose neither? How is the choice to not make a choice any different from the quasi-comatose behavior exhibited in an institution, where all choices were made for the individual and the only choice was whether to exist or not? This compromises the integrity. The diminution of the essential truth. In some ways, to teach lying, denial of self and truth. At what point do we punish them for their delusional behavior? Are we so much better off with our keen intellects and supreme free will? Unfettered access in our information age. Limited only by the powers of our own imagination, so the advertisements tell us. What a load of rubbish. I think people make too much fuss about choices. We place too much pride in our free will, when really . . .

I must remember to call Mr. Black. The others need me to save them from their miserable lots in life. Only my unwavering will shall lead them to the promised land, where art is worshipped. I, Ass Cream Man, shall part the red sea of inflammation and constipation and deliver my people, unscathed, to a big bunch of sand, where we shall wander for a great long time. But we shall be free. Hooray for me!

Richard's disintegration was not really a surprise. After all, there's only so much memory. Can the entire history really be embedded in this new technology? Still, one becomes attached after a certain period of time. Perhaps, it's just the familiarity. I'd like to think it was more than just that. Man of woman born, and all men must die, and all those things. But is manhood defined by behavior or phallus or chromosomes? All of the above? And when are things not what they seem? When man is sissy? When man is prosperous? When man is machine? What then?

If I were to tell you what Richard's last words were, you would not believe me. Richard's last words. Some would argue that the long hours he spent logged on were to blame. Fourteen to sixteen hours per day in his basement, just wired. Or perhaps his roommate, who ended up killing herself. In the attic. With a rope. Only to be discovered by Professor Plum. His skin was so pale after not leaving the house for days. I think it was the lack of flesh and bone contact, but I, of course, would think that. I wanted this movie to save us. If not to save, then at least to bring us back to the days in high school, when we would sit in my parents' basement and plot our revolutions. I wanted all things to once again seem possible. No compromises. No retreat, baby, and no surrender.

Richard desired to be buried in Nova Scotia. In a small cemetery near the ocean. The wind blows across the rocks and the beach and through my hair. The sky gray and thick. The sea would be such a pleasant place to be buried. Too bad most people end up in a box in the ground. At least it wasn't a computer shipping box, like he'd always joked about. I think in the end, he wanted to be free from all that. When we were fresh away from college and he was still living in Ann Arbor, in an attic, we were lying down on the floor at 3:00 A.M., drunk from words, I asked him how he wanted to be remembered.

He got all serious and said, "I don't."

I promised I would write a book about him to guarantee that he would be forgotten. (Now that I am doing that, I take no joy in killing off my best friend before he has had his glorious day in the sun. Still, art's a bitch.) We fell asleep soon after that. He had already left for work in the engineering computer lab when I awoke. I spent the rest of the day reading the *Sunday NY Times* and eating bagels at Ernie's Deli on State Street. The sun was thick so that all my bones became pure.

David's Requiem

I got up again at 3:20 A.M. and my heart was pounding. I sat in the green-upholstered easy chair and stared at the window in the van house. Before I go to bed each night, I am sure to plan how the intruders are going to break in through the front window, rape my wife, and then kill her while I am forced to watch at gunpoint. My arms would be broken behind my back. They shoot me in the leg and I lay bleeding while they shit on the bed. They don't take anything, but they turn over furniture and rip up my New Directions paperbacks, and scatter the pages in every room of the house. I don't bother to call out. I just lay there, waiting to die. It takes me hours to die and I refuse to remember anything so I merely count the seconds. I could count tenths of seconds if I could. I still remembered.

I am above my body, floating now, and I am calm. I am only bleeding and she, my wife, is only sleeping. Her face is still on her head and she is only dreaming.

Perhaps we will go dancing tomorrow. She will wear her

black dress and white pearls. Her hair is down and she is radiant in the gray of dusk. I am wearing my gray suit and paisley-red tie. We are striking together and everybody turns to look as we enter the dance hall.

I can hear my hear beating. It is in my eardrum. My throat is open and I am thirsty.

I hadn't spoken to Richard or Stephen for several months since I'd gone back to school. I know Stephen was in Calgary, working on that TV show. Richard was supposedly doing whatever it is that he does. But making a zillion bucks doing it. All are happy.

Happy.

Superhappy.

Happy happy.

I woke up tired today. My eyes are still bleary. I'm waiting for the gal in the next cube to start her coffee maker. It's about eighty-four degrees and absolutely no fresh air. My ears are red. The lady in the next cube is listening to some shitty rap music. God, that just sucks. I wish they would turn on the air conditioner. Budget cuts.

I am thumbing through some shitty self-help book I stole off someone's desk. Not the lady who called in sick and drove three hours to Indiana to buy a hundred bucks' worth of lottery tickets. I told her she might as well just give it to me for all she is going to get out of the deal. She didn't think it was funny. I also told her I hoped she got struck by lightning. That would be a good sign. She didn't think it was funny. I told her that I read in the paper that she has better odds of breaking her mother's back by stepping on a crack. She didn't think it was funny.

This was a different lady who told me that she would never let her children be watched by a man, even a family member, because all men are potential child molesters. I said by that line of reasoning, you should kill your male children so they don't molest their children when they get older. She didn't laugh. I continued that I thought that she was right and that was probably what God was trying to tell Abraham when he wanted him to sacrifice Isaac. She, being a good Baptist, changed the subject to talk about how a previous manager who worked there was gay and shouldn't be allowed to adopt a child because he's sick. I asked her if it was the Bible or some other book that talked about throwing the first stone, and about love above all, and other kind of stuff and she quoted some stupid stuff back at me so I had to spit at her.

It wasn't from the desk of the other lady, who told me about the secret tunnels underneath Detroit. I asked if she meant the salt mines or the sewers. She said, "Oh no, the tunnels. The white folks have tunnels under the city so that they can kill black folk and make a quick getaway." The tunnels apparently go underneath all several hundred thousand homes throughout the dozens of square miles that are the city of Detroit. She said oh yeah, that the preacher had mentioned it at church and that is why the white people don't want the black people to get casinos. I just smiled and said "Oh really?" This woman incidentally has an MBA.

A Note from Liz

After visiting Boston and Cambridge, it is difficult to see how it is the hub of Massachusetts, let alone the universe, or whatever that silly slogan is. It has the same stores and such as those located in Metro Detroit. The parks look nicer in films. Not one of the many colleges or universities in the area has produced a national championship football team. Not one. I will go as far as saying the last thing of any relevance to come from the entire East Coast in the last fifty years was that movie about the math guy—the black-and-white one—not the Rocky type one.

Note to Stephen prior to our departure.

Hey, Stephen.

How's it going? Life here is swell. Liz's dahlias are in full bloom and the yard is full of them. I'm plugging away at the novel in fits and spurts, and some days are better than others, you know. How's life at the "other school?" Are you a robot yet? We're coming out that way the last week in August. Perhaps we could get lunch?

Love, David.

Several days later, the response came via e-mail.
Call me when you get here—S.

This reminded me of how much I hate e-mail. There's just not enough data to know if he meant "Sounds good, I am excited you're finally coming to Boston, we must see each other." Did he mean "Yeah, whatever." Or "I'll believe you guys will actually follow through and leave the city of Dearborn when I am pinching your flesh in the Middle East and tabouli is stuck in your tooth."

I wrote his number down in several notebooks and in the front cover of the Romer's Guide so that I couldn't lose it. The night before we left, I was so jazzed with going that I only slept four hours. The third time, I got up and made the rounds, chucking the window upstairs, then the windows downstairs, pausing to look at the back window in the study for a few minutes, wondering if the cops would ever bust those freaks for burning tires in their backyard. I read for few minutes from *On Being A Person* and wondered if one of the infallible universal truths of existence was of man's need for relationships. Meaningful in the sense of warmth, congruence, positive regard, and the one true experience of this is in one's relationship to God.

Several years ago we were in Chicago, eating breakfast at 3:00 A.M. in some little dive in Wrigleyville, past the public housing and the parking lot. I had oatmeal and wheat toast, of course. We were all drinking regular coffee by the pot back then.

The conversation:

Stephen: So anyway, I was with my roommate, Vic, and we were leaving the bar at like 3:30 A.M. and these two guys cross over the street and come up to us and started getting in our face. Like, hey, did you bump into me for any reason, asshole? And I'm thinking what are these assholes saying, they weren't even in the bar—you would have remembered them—gold rope chains, leather coats, sunglasses, corn rows—real bangers, you know. Vic's all apologetic and everything and they're like, "Maybe you should give us blowjobs to let us know how sorry you are." I go to him, "Fuck yourself, Coolio." The next thing you know, their friend pulls up unto the sidewalk and jumps me and gets my arms behind my back, and they are just beating the shit out of me right on the street. I'm bleeding from my nose and mouth and just dying for sure right there on the street. My eye was swollen shut for three days and I had a detached retina.

Liz: That's awful, you could have been killed.

David: Did you call the cops?

Richard: More importantly, did you at least get in some good licks?

Stephen: They kicked our asses. I didn't throw a single punch. I was on my knees and they were punishing our asses.

Richard: That's why you should always carry mace.

Stephen: If I would have tried that, they would have shoved it right into my anus, I am sure.

Richard: You cant' let people push you around like that, Stephen. That's why I'm studying the ancient martial art of tae kwon do. No one is going to mess with me like that.

Stephen: Richard, these dudes had guns. They would have capped us. They were just pounding us for fun. For something to do to pass the time.

But in a weird way, I deserved it.

Liz: Bullshit. What do you mean you deserved it?

Stephen: Because my father was such a racist.

Liz: Are you joking? Is this a put-on or what? You've got to be kidding.

No reply.

Richard: Well, that reminds me of when I was at the grocery store one time. This guy in front of me had seventeen items and the sign said "Express 15 items or less," you know. So I tapped the guy on the shoulder and said, "Excuse me, you have too many items." He just looked away. So I picked up his carton of eggs and threw them on the ground.

David: Did you really?

Richard: Oh yeah. I refuse to let people take advantage of me.

David: So what happened?

Richard: Oh, you know, they called over a security guard and had me taken out and all that bullshit. But who cares? It's the principle of the thing.

Liz: But you didn't even get your groceries!

Richard: No, Liz, but I kept my self-respect. My point is there are absolute, non-negotiable things of supreme value, and these are things which compel us to act.

David: Is the error of the other man perhaps a simple counting error? Perhaps, even a counting error on your part? Is your destruction of property and personal aggression justified?

Richard: Tyranny must never be ignored. That's what you postmodern Marxists don't understand.

Richard: Of course knew that I was neither a Marxist nor a postmodernist, but he still managed to get my goat.

David: Surely you are not comparing one simple act, even if was purposive, still just an act between two individuals, not comparing it to the systemic oppression and exclusion of the minority group by the white majority?

Richard: This is how it starts. The Holocaust did not start with Auschwitz, David, it did not start with Kristallnacht. It did not start with the 1936 Olympics. It started because one man hated other men because of perceived inequities.

David: If I was really postmodernist, I'd have something really absurd and biting to say about this argument, as well as about the Holocaust. But I'm not, and I'm tired.

Liz: You know that all logic left our debate about the time when you, Richard, threw the eggs on the ground.

Richard laughed. We all laughed. I knew it wasn't about logic. It never was.

The Eyes—David Lying on the Couch:

The eyes, the eyes, the eyes. I'm so sick and tired about the goddamn eyes. His eyes were no different before or after the whole thing. Primo or posto. Ante or exte. They just did not change. And I'm not saying this is due to some character flaw. That he was a heartless such and such or something. I'm just saying I think there's way too big a deal made about the eyes.
Other Voice: But he didn't cry?
David: That's what I'm saying. But why does that bother me so much?
Other Voice: What makes you say that? Because he was not blubbering all over himself, like you did?
David: Well, no, I did not seem to cry at the funeral per se. But who cares? There's more than one way to experience an event, you should know that.
Other Voice: Should I?
David: I'm sure at some point, he had cried so fucking much it would have made you ashamed to even be having this conversation with me. I'm sure you would just shrivel in that little head of yours and disappear.
Other Voice: Maybe. What about the speech?
David: It was beautiful. It was poetic. It was inspiring, it was honest, it was sad. No one walked away unmoved.
Other Voice: No one?
David: What do you want me to say? That it was the worst display of showmanship ever? That because he was an actor, that he doesn't feel, that he doesn't experience pain? What is that? That it was some kind of an act? That nonsense, just completely and utter nonsense? The eyes. I think we see in the eyes the things we desire to see. Yes. I think the eyes of the others are wired into our soul or our psyche. We, in longing, we seek unity with these eyes, which will revive us, which are sympathetic to our needs. The eyes are just rods and cones and rods and cones. The rest is just us.

Colin lay in his bed.

The morning light was gray and slumbering through the window. He rubbed his eyes, but they would not focus. The bedroom furniture, the dresser, the chair. Everything was different. Not in pattern or color or location, but different still. He was filled with memories of being alone and being trapped in his bedroom with the monsters lurking outside the door. The saliva and the stench of urine soaking his bed. His eyes were now outside, his head floating in the gray light. The chair has memories of being alone as a child and being with the monsters. The chair has memories too, he knows, and the gray air was coming in like a blanket to smother the memories. If there was some way to fight the gray air. To repel the light from entering the room. Colin took the blanket from the closet and draped it over the curtain too, and pressed it desperately over the pane. He smiled and sat on the bed. His plan appeared to be working, the room was dark and the gray light was in the chair in the black room. He rubbed the gray memories all over his body like a salve. A "Salve Regina." Even the dirt memories of dirt in mammary were pretty now inside the room, in the gray, in the chair. The flesh is the fabric, is the crystallized thought. The sheets are like bones and would, too, turn to dust. The bed too, would soon be memories, and they would be called Colin Darden.

David

I woke up at 12:54 A.M. I walked down the stairs to go to the bathroom. I stood in the darkness, unblinking. I pinched myself. I was not dead, as I thought I might be. I urinated. I was not murdered. I was not. I could shoot an arrow through, too. I am the hero. Fuck Stephen. It's my fucking book. I rubbed my eyes and walked off the cross. My eyes rolled before me. Leading the way.

"Why are you calling out to me?"

"What?"
"Hold up your staff. Hold up your rod."
"My rod?"
"Your rod. It is a weapon of God."
"What?"
"Perhaps you are not the one."

I stepped on my eyes and killed them. They are sorry little bastards anyway. Why does Stephen always get to be the martyr?

No Junk

Richard was sitting in the Ann Arbor Public Library, reading *The Confessions of St. Augustine* when it hit him. God don't make no junk.

Liz and I got into this dispute.

L: Maybe we should think about selling the house and moving to Paris.
D: What?
L: Yeah, you hate your job, I hate my job. We're both sick of the MOTOR CITY.
D: Yeah, but . . . the house . . . my student loans . . .
L: Well, we'd still have to work. But we'd sell the house, we'd make money on it. We could live on that.
D: Yeah, for how long? What about the money I owe my dad for that stupid film?
L: David, he doesn't really expect you to pay him back. You know that.
D: Still . . . Paris. Neither of us speak French . . .
L: You speak Spanish. We could learn French. People have done it—
D: Liz, are you joking? I'm surprised to hear you saying this. Paris . . . I mean, we've talked about it and talked about it, but we're thirty years old. What—are we just going to start a new life? I mean in a foreign country? We've never even

been to Europe—the farthest we've been was Toronto . . . and you remember that . . . we went to that jazz club and the band was from Detroit, so that doesn't even count.
L: Maybe you're right.
D: (pause) Are you serious about this? What happened at work? Did that janitor hit on you again?
L: No, I just am so sick of feeling tired every time I come home. I feel so old.
D: Maybe we should have kids.
L: You're kidding, right?
D: Ummm, no.
L: David, you know we're not going to bring kids into this freaking world so they can get sodomized by the next-door neighbor or whatever . . . besides, you don't just wipe away your angst by having a kid. That's no answer.
D: Maybe it is, Liz. Maybe that angst is just the little signal saying "Hey, have a kid."
L: I don't think so. Hey, are we going out for dinner or what? I'm getting hungry
D: Thai Kitchen?
L: Sounds good. I have to pee first.

After the Gold Rush

Stephen came back from California a changed man. At least, that's what Liz thought. I disagreed, but she had the evidence so I couldn't get her to budge; she was that way. She blamed it all on the corrupting influence of Mr. Black. I told her she was too hard on people, especially Stephen, and that she should have some sympathy on him. "He's going through a rough time of it, trying to get his bearings straight. I mean, losing your dad will do that to you."

I didn't need to finish. She had been there. The Mexican restaurant. The margaritas, the low-cal salad dressing and the tortilla chips, leaving the grease pools on the wax paper. The odd pitch to his voice and the intonation. For God's sake, you've lived in California for one month. But we heard the stories:

— The make-out with the junior starlet at some C-list party.
— The gay roommate gay-sexing some aging TV star on the kitchen floor.
— The cocaine and pancake breakfast with M—K—
— The threesome with the transvestite and the stripper.
— Etc.
— Etc.
— The auditions with S—
— The boob jobs which are so disgusting but so "necessary."

Damning Richard for his celibacy. Smugly insinuating we are dullards because we are married. We are dullards and we are married. There is a correlation but not causation, you bastard. Chastising my mood swings and my fear of Paris. But who am I to judge? He says, "Who am I to judge?"

"I'm still just a kid from the Midwest."

He said this, I swear to God in all seriousness.

Do you remember how in *My Dinner with Andre*, you loved it for the great film it is, but sometimes you couldn't believe how pretentious Andre was, and you kind of just wanted to smack him?

At least Andre was trying to communicate to something that was larger than himself, larger than just silly, silly, adolescent-type behavior, for God's sake.

"People out there are so open-minded. God, the sunshine, it's . . . I mean I was at the beach just yesterday, learning to surf. Can you believe it? Surfing in October, for God's sake. I come here, I have to wear a sweater." He lowered his voice to a whisper. "And I have got people excited about the film. They are so into it, it's scary. Mr. Black took me to a meeting and people were practically giving me blank checks. It was like some movie or something."

I had to admit I was getting excited. I had another crummy day at work, one of my clients was evicted, another had their insurance cut off, and another got arrested for selling crack. I felt like Sisyphus. And now, here comes Stephen, spinning his web....

"So, how much did you get?" Liz asked.

"What do you mean?" Stephen replied.

"What do you mean, what do I mean? I mean, how much cash did you get for the movie?"

"Well, none really. But Liz, that's not the way it works out there. They don't just give you the money to make any film you want. They need more than just an idea and a promise. Especially when you're talking about it being written by some unknowns from Detroit. I mean, yeah, people recognize me there, and they like my work, but it's one thing to get cast in some good commercials. It's a whole other story to talk about getting a project green-lighted."

Liz stared at him icily. She didn't have to say what was on her mind. We could all feel it. She was just throwing out these anger rays from her eyeballs that were enough to scare the bejeebies out of me, and I loved her. Poor Stephen.

"So, do you ever wish you hadn't been kicked out of Harvard?" she asked. I was pretty sure she didn't want an answer.

"Do you ever wish you hadn't been kicked out of the band that you started?" Stephen said.

I knew where this was headed and did my best to steer it to a better place.

"So, I hear Richard likes his knew job at the Defense Department," I said.

"He's wasting his time," Stephen and Liz said together.

"He's too talented for that," Stephen added.

"He's too creative. He's this brilliant cyber-poet guy and he's working on some stupid government database thing," Liz said.

"Well, you gotta pay the bills, I suppose," I said.

"Funny for you to say that, Mr. 'An artist should never get paid for his art,'" Liz said.

"Well, isn't this a fun way to spend an evening?" I said to no one in particular. Hoping that the waitress would come with our check soon, so I could go home and read the newspaper, or go through the pile of bills that was beginning to collect dust on my dining room table.

Psychosis Disorder, NOS

Richard may have become completely psychotic at some point, or it could be another joke. Another 3:00 A.M. phone call with another theory. He indicated that the Epictetus scene in *Portrait* was not written by Joyce, but by Henry McKay, a southern political cartoonist living in London. "Joyce's attempt to use Epictetus was a dividing line between youth and senility that he is not being truthful. Stephen distances himself from the Stoic, calling him who said 'Let us enjoy the banquet of life with other men.' If Joyce would not have realized that Stephen's whole desire was to be the poet of the ages and to create the conscience of his entire race, is not the evidence clear, and why would Joyce be as sloppy as all that?"

I answered that Stephen/Joyce's desire to disavow his heritage was the guilt of him not visiting his dying mother to reunite to become whole. He was trying to resolve himself of the guilt. By exiling. Richard called me on this psychobabble bullshit and we agreed that the whole thing was not worth discussing. He said he needed to tape our conversation for use in the movie. I still that we should try writing a script or something so we don't get bogged down in so much proselytizing bullshit. Sometimes, Richard would get all affected and such and I would want to smack him. Richard, you coy boy. All this Epictetus and such. Mostly, I was just tired and knew that neither of us really had a clue what we were talking about. Not that it should have stopped us from saying it. But perhaps, at a more reasonable hour. I had an exam tomorrow night for my Theories of Counseling class, and I would be too busy at work to study.

"Good night, Richard," I said.

"Wait, this is important. We have to get this stuff ironed out so we can get the script done."

"Are we back to using a script? I thought we were doing the improvisational thing."

"No, no, no. Don't you and Stephen ever talk about this stuff? Mr. Black wants a script. I think he's right. I haven't been too happy with this whole 'first thought/best thought' school of filmmaking."

"It's so much more real . . ."

"It's garbage. Just a bunch of gobbledygook and indecipherable gee-wizardry."

"All right, but can we talk about it at a reasonable hour? I'm really very tired."

"Okay, okay, good night, but I'll call you tomorrow."

"Good night."

I tried falling back to sleep, deep breathing, imagery of the ocean and all that, but couldn't. He had set my mind reeling again. The thought of sitting in a room listening to people's problems all day was becoming less and less like a good career move, especially because on a macro level, I don't really approve of people. I spent many sessions with my therapist trying to resolve this. He told me to keep a journal about it. I have been, but am worried that I will come home from work and see the ATF dragging out my computer and boxes of notebooks.

I went downstairs, grabbed a rough edit of the film from the top of the pile and popped it in the VCR. I sat in the dark, watching the footage of James Joyce riding his bicycle through Paris, legs pedaling quickly, swerving around other cyclists, Django Reinhart on the soundtrack. Then the slow dissolve to Colin sitting on his brown corduroy recliner, medium shot, his face gray and sunken, licking his cracked lips. His hand quivering as he thumbs through the big brown book. A slight nod and a smile as he finds the page where he had last left off. He begins in a rich Irish baritone, its musical lilt belying the strain that his lungs must have felt with each breath.

I began crying. God, I missed him. I wanted to call my own father and wake him up and see if he wanted to go shoot pool or go to see a baseball game, or just to tell him I love him, but at

3:30 A.M., I thought the better of it. I heard Liz coming down the stairs and started coughing to try to hide the fact that I was crying. She didn't say anything, just came and sat on my lap, with her arms around my neck. After a moment, she gave me a kiss on the cheek. We watched for a few minutes in silence as the words rolled over us, like the warm gentle waves off Cape Hatteras, thankful that there was at least, for a moment, a witness to each other's existence in the universe.

Verbal Manslaughter

Richard called again. He got fired from his job at the Department of Defense. Apparently, he scored lowest in the DD54 psychological profile of anyone in the history of the test administration. I tried to reassure him by telling him there were no third-generation, Albanian-American, left-handed bisexuals in the normative sample. But he was not reassured.

"They need a little visit from the postman," I said.

He forced a chuckle.

"Richard, you just need to go a little whoopass on them, that's all."

His voice was tired at first, then rising in pitch and volume. "God, this whole thing is just bullshit, you know. I mean, goddamn. I've worked there for over a year and totally streamlined the data retrieval process. I'm saving them like forty million a year, you know. And this, this stupid goddamn test. David, you know what bullshit these things are. All computer-scored and artificial cut-offs, and it's just so irrelevant. And so am I, in their eyes, at least. But I'm not. I got shit on them. I swear to God I got serious shit on them."

I could hear some voices in the background.

"Richard, are you all right?"

Then click. The phone went dead.

I called back right away but the phone kept ringing.

That's Richard, I thought, and went to bed.

I woke up the next morning with sunlight warming my face.

God, it felt so good. Soft and delicious on my skin. I didn't want to leave the bed. Just melt into it—losing my bones and flesh and my nervous system. Retrogress. Heartbeat. Heartbeat. Then give up the need for sickness. Embrace the heat of the sun to be the one, the same of life and light.

Then the shrill voice of a mortal interrupts me.

"Goddammit, David, come downstairs quick. Wake up. Richard's in trouble."

In a snap, my eyes open and I become aware of my body as I stubbed my toe on the bedrail. By the first step, I recall the phone call from last night and its abrupt ending. I was lucid despite my bloody toe and panic.

Liz, breathless, a step in front. "He's on TV. He was arrested."

"Arrested. Holy shit, what for?"

By this time, we were down the stairs and standing before a snapshot of Richard in the upper corner of the television screen, floating without a body above the talking head.

The feed: "Richard Miscovich, recently fired from the Department of Defense, was arrested last night on charges of verbal manslaughter stemming from negative comments he made against his former employer. He is the first person charged under the recently passed Jackson Act authored by Republican Congressman from Georgia, Andrew Jefferson Jackson III."

"I can't believe it, Liz, this is absurd."

"Where do you think they took him?"

"I don't know. Would they have taken him to the county jail? Probably not."

"God, no. I'll bet they took him to some federal holding tank somewhere. God. Poor Richard. Poor little Richard. He'll kill himself . . . I know he will. He can't handle this kind of bullshit. Not now."

My head was swimming now and I had to sit down, regretting my inability to disappear into the sunlight. Liz went into the kitchen and returned with a couple of cups of coffee. She handed me a cup.

"Here, this'll make you feel better."

I reached for the cup but had a hard time feeling the cup. They were shaking and she put pressure on my hand to help hold it steady. We raised the cup to my lips and I sipped. I think I began crying.

"We have to move to Halifax. Let's leave now," I said.

"I know, I know, it's awful. God, I know. But Richard . . ."

"He'll be dead any minute. If he's not already."

She moved the hair from my eyes.

"We can't let those bastards get away with this," she whispered. She had a steady look in her eyes and I knew she was right.

How that whack-o got that bill through, I'll never know. I'm so sick of those pathetic Democrats.

The next few days were a flurry of activity. I called everyone I knew who I thought could possibly help with this. Senators and congressman. State and federal. The mayor, the president, the Secretary of Defense, the Secretary of the Interior and their secretaries. I called Richard's boss, and my friend, Fred, who was an attorney with Legal Aid. I called the ACLU, the NEA, the NRA, and the NFL—they agreed to do something about the disturbing inability of many safeties to make an open field tackle. I called the phone company, and I called the cable company. I quickly set up a website, a phone bank, and created a non-profit organization, "Free Rico" (I thought the intimation that he was an oppressed migrant worker or president of Guatemala might help our cause. Liz was on the *Today Show* the next morning and was brilliant. She looked dazzling, and she made the government's attorney weep openly, apparently a *Today Show* first. I did a radio interview for an underground newspaper in the fascist republic of Devonshire, and was sure to get in a plug for our film. We had the cameras rolling nonstop. We knew we had killer footage.

In the end, we were too effective. We were hoping to get some excellent feed from *Supreme Court TV*. It was rumoured the chief justice was finally going to get his way and all participants would be forced to wear those silly wigs, like they do in the

United Kingdom of Great Britain and Northern Ireland. Sorry, it's been so long since I mentioned Ireland, I've been awfully remiss in my revising responsibilities. Did you notice that I at least spelled "rumoured" the funny (British) way? But in the end, the government was forced to drop their case.

Not that they realized that there was absolutely no way "under God's green earth," as my Polish grandmother used to say, mixing her metaphors as quickly as she mixed her dough for pierogis, that the constitutionality of a law based on "the use of foul language, or the appearance of the use of foul or unkind language, directed by a person in an inferior capacity towards one's superiors or persons in charge of the other person, or people with significantly more money or prestige than the other person, so that the party of the second part might in some way be offended, and realizing that a mere civil suit would not be warranted due to the aggressor's lack of financial resources to plunder . . ." I swear to God, the word "plunder" is actually in this bill, check it out yourself: HR 101.9. No, it wasn't because of that. It was simply because apparently, the bill's author, Senator Jefferson, made naughty comments about the president, who found the mechanisms of law to be too torpid in their resolution of this injustice, and had the senator's brakes removed from his automobile, resulting in a dramatic change of heart from the Intensive Care Unit of Fairfax County Memorial Hospital, and a moving speech involving the words, "Regret, liberty, small children and puppy dogs, American flag, healing power of Jesus." Lastly, he confessed tearfully, "I have come to accept that I may have in the past occasionally conducted myself in a manner that could possibly be construed as mildly unkind, or hurtful to people who can't really take a joke, or who are too insensitive to realize that I had a very difficult childhood. Please forgive me."

Richard was released ten minutes after the hospital bed confession. He looked great. He had received a tattoo of Herve Vellechez and grown a goatee. He looked like he had put on a few pounds, mostly muscle.

"I lifted a lot of weights," he said after I asked him about it.

"What was it like? It must have been awful," Liz said.

"It wasn't that bad really. I met some really nice folks, people a lot like us, except for maybe their selling crack or capping someone . . . but I mean . . . real people. There was one guy who gave me some really good ideas for the film. Apparently, he was president of the James Joyce Fan Club in Texas, before the little run-in with the law."

"The run-in?"

"I guess some guy was really trashed and talking smack about JJ. He had this really crazy theory that Joyce's vision problems were a ruse, a lie, just a publicity stunt that he and Pound concocted. Almost like a way to get chicks or something. My friend, William, had known this; I mean it's like common knowledge, right? But where William took offense was when the guy said that *Finnegan's Wake* might as well have been written by a blind man, as obtuse as it is. This is where William couldn't control his temper and punched the man in the nose."

"He's in jail in Virginia for punching someone in the nose in Texas?"

"Well, no, he killed some people, but it had nothing to do with James Joyce."

"Thank God for that." Liz said.

"Did you happen to get any of that on tape?" I asked.

"Sorry, but I'm sure we can re-enact it. William looked a lot like Alice B. Toklas, so we can have you play him, David."

"Most amusing, you little felon, you."

We walked the eight blocks to Richard's apartment, enjoying the crisp October breeze. We didn't have much to say, so we began singing the score from *The Music Man*, but I couldn't keep up. After, a terrible version of *Till There Was You*, which Richard and Liz serenaded me with, I gave up. For once, their shenanigans did not annoy the crap out of me. I lagged behind and enjoyed looking at the moon rising above the row houses, the moon so thin and white, content.

Real-Time Update

Did you know that there are many people in America who harbor suspicion and unkind thoughts to people who are different from them? It's true! Perhaps, if we all were a bit nicer to each other, the world would be a much happier place. In an effort at balance, what if Trent Lott was right, what if Strom Thurmond would have been a great president? *** If you look at the number of African-American males whose address involves a cell block number, perhaps we might consider that the government to date have not been very successful at extending the benefits of democracy to all of her children.

***Of course, I personally don't believe this as I listen to National Public Radio, subscribe to the *Washington Post Weekly Edition*, belong to a union and all the other LIBERAL bona fides (plus I am not a fucking idiot). Still, in a free society with a FREE PRESS, shouldn't someone at least make an effort to have a dialogue on this issue, instead of everybody using every goddamn thing to push their own agenda, advance their own career?

Note to editor (self): I think you might be right. If the wire services pick up on this, I'm bound to get some ink and sell a few more books. Cha-ching!

My next-door neighbor, DA Peckerhead, recently smashed his car due to doing "something kind of dumb." He said "drunk driving." Of course, neither of these impediments has stopped him from driving. He can currently be seen driving to the party store, with his front bumper attached to his car in a curious combination of duct tape and rope. This incident has provided him with the necessary motivation to bang on the metal portions of his car at 11:00 P.M. while listening to all types of great music created by Brian Johnson, era AC/DC and Stone Temple Pilots. My two-year-old daughter, after hearing one of the catchy hymns, asked what hell it was. I told her that we were there now and it wasn't as bad as I thought it would be, but she didn't laugh.

There are fourteen individuals in my zip code that are listed on the State of Michigan's sex-offender registry web site. The nearest one, an individual convicted of CSC III, lives two blocks from our house. He rides around the neighborhood with a baby seat on his bike. When he gets out the clown suit, we're out of here. In the zip code where I was born and lived the first twenty-three years of my life, there are forty-three registered sex offenders. In Huntington Woods, there are none. Part of me feels ashamed for taking the time and emotional energy to think about this. Isn't this just making me more afraid, more judgmental, more cynical about the human race? Is this knowledge really going to help me be a better parent, a better protector of my daughter and soon-to-be-born son? What would Jesus drive? I haven't come to any resolution about this. But as I kneel at my daughter's bedside and say prayers with her, I know I'm not really praying for her to make it through the night, but to make it through the day, when I'm not there to hover over her. To make it through the day, when she has to let go of my hand and walk to school herself, or ride her bike to her friend's house. And I'm praying for my wife and I to believe that we won't lose our minds worrying about it.

The Drawer of Drawers

The task of cleaning out a dead father's underwear drawer is never a pleasant one. The idea of going through a dead person's stuff is just straight-out creepy, first of all. I mean, the person once wore these underpants, but now does not. What's up with that? Next, one is likely to have a somewhat emotional reaction when one realizes the white briefs one is folding were your father's, and he's dead, and you miss him like hell. You miss the times you came home from school after soccer practice and he'd have roast beef stew and tea, seated at the coffee table in the living room, and he'd be cursing at Tom Brokaw for not opening his mouth when he talked. Then you too would get into a discussion about the current event—likely a tax issue, and it would end up into a history lesson of how Michael O'Flannan was a great man and how those stupid Brits were ruining the whole goddamn island. Maybe, with the stupid Yanks and the dirty Jews, we'd all be dead in a year, or all enslaved. Of course you would argue back, attacking his bizarre conspiratorial outlook and his bigoted comments, which he could never adequately defend, and you would occasionally use a big word to try to put him in his place because you were an Advanced Placement, college-bound student, and he was after all a fucking printer, an ink boy, and he didn't even finish secondary school. But he would call you bullshit and chastise you for your pernicious and odious ways, mostly for your arrogance, and then you would turn on *Jeopardy* and solve the questions together. And then at the bottom, underneath the socks, you find this.

A GREAT NOVEL IN PROGRESS

by Colin Darden

"I didn't want to write this book. I really haven't had an interest in writing a novel, finding most of them too insufferably long and meandering (before 1950) or too cloy and self-referential, or self-conscious and both, since about 1992, and let's just forget about the ones in between those years. One might say I am too cynical and self-important for my own good, therefore, I am the perfect candidate to write a compelling contemporary NOVEL (like this word has any meaning whatsoever), or better yet, they tell me to write a MEMOIR, which is a novel for those too lazy to make up stuff. For God's sake, life is tough all over, get over it. There are like maybe a dozen people in the world who have the right to write a memoir, and only half of those are living at this moment, and half of that half could actually put a few sentences together. Those that have done it, and done it well (like Miriam Winter), make anyone who ever thought about writing anything at all, let alone a memoir, want to cut off their hands and poke out their eyeballs (slick foreshadowing).

Mostly, I haven't written a novel or a memoir-y type thing before because I've been too busy as a transgendered, transsexual,

Asian immigrant priest and Mafioso, who was a Holocaust survivor as well as a Vietnam veteran, to sit down and write a bunch of silly words on a page. And then throw in my stint as a steamboat captain, professional gambler, unwed teen mother, first man on the moon, rock star, fireman, and billionaire, and you can see my interests lie elsewhere. I know I don't have to mention that I graduated from Harvard, but I didn't walk during commencement—those philistines. I also adore golden retriever puppies and long walks in the summer rain.

Anyway, one day, I was at a café in Budapest and my personal assistant was pouring cream into my cappuccino, and he said, "Luigi, you are such a complex and fascinating man, perhaps you could share some of your adventures with the rest of us to provide some respite from the extremely small and empty lives that we lead."

I must admit I have a keen sense of responsibility to give back to the little people and let them know that if they work hard and give 110 percent, they too can be as successful as I have become. Still, my modesty, which many say is my most attractive quality, kept me from seriously considering such a thing. I mean, who would be interested in my story, fantastic as it may be? After all, I am but a man. My personal assistant, my longtime confidant and dear friend, his name escapes me at the moment, is above all, persistent. He asked me at least one or two times before I finally acquiesced. His final argument, that I could possibly develop a movie based on my book as well as inspire a whole generation of young people to forsake caffeine, attend mass daily, and revive Latin as the language of choice in most American households, just like it was in 1933, before television and its commie Jew infrastructure destroyed our great nation and caused the great Stock Market Crash and the invasion of Pearl Harbor; that was enough to convince me to try to write a book.

Let me rephrase—that was enough to convince me to successfully write a great book. Do you see what I did there? Let me point out how I adroitly rewrote that last clause to eliminate the word "try." This shows two things—one, that I am a great writer because I am self-critical and read page three of the book *How To Write A GREAT BOOK TODAY*, where it says, rule #1 "REVISE, REVISE, REVISE," which I interpreted to mean that one should revise one's work. It also echoes a great philosopher, I think it was Wittenberg who said, "Try? There is no try, do or do not." In fact, this proverb has been a source of great inspiration to me throughout my many travails. I will try to share as many of these important philosophical nuggets as I can, as well as explain them, as I am sure many of you will not quite understand them, although you will lie to yourself and nod your head with great pride, pretending you do—believe me, you don't. I also will include a glossary at the end of the book to help you look up many of the words I use, as I use a great many difficult words, being an *entomophilies* (Latin for lover of words) and scoring a 710 on the GRE verbal section, I simply can't help but infuse my prose with uxorious semantics. I also know that many of you who don't live in New York City do not own dictionaries, and the public library in your very small towns keeps both irregular hours and abridged dictionaries. Sorry if I sound so condescending, but when it comes to abridgement, I can't help but develop an air of smug superiority. I own the *New Shorter Oxford Dictionary* and find myself spending many an afternoon perusing it, looking up new words, and the twelfth to seventeenth entries for words that are familiar to most plebeians.

But do you know what? I am very bad at Scrabble. In fact, if you were to develop a complex rating scale as I did that considers one's household income, IQ, length of last marlin caught, while factoring in number of languages spoken to determine a Scrabble handicap, I may be the world's worst Scrabble player. No joke. My wife, Greta, and I were spending last New Year's Day at the Renaissance Weekend, playing Scrabble with our friends, Hil and Bill, and I got trounced (a seventeen-point word—where were you when I needed you?). Actually, it was a couples match and Greta and I were flummoxed. This is interesting because Greta, the second-greatest writer in my house (and of her generation), who also teaches calculus to Brazilian street children during summer holiday, sucks at Scrabble. I am thinking about developing a paper to present at the next Modern Language Association Conference explaining my theory about my Scrabble Handicap System and its theoretical underpinnings (thanks to Herr Doktor Van Hoffman for the help with the string theory lit search). However, as I know many of you (I'm just being nice here) won't attend this conference, let me simplify this. You don't have to be smart to be good at Scrabble. The corollary: Not all smart people are good at Scrabble. I would also like to highlight Luigi Rule #1: You can still be successful in certain areas, even if you have limitations or weaknesses in other areas of your life. Although the more weaknesses you have relative to strengths, the more you deserve the meager spoils that you dig through rubbish piles for and which you embrace as victories, which for you, perhaps they are. I believe it was the great Levitical scholar Israel Ben Ben who reminds us, "God hates weakness, those who have significant personality deficits shall be exiled by Him." I'm not sure that helps, but I am receiving a large stipend from the Society for the Advancement of Judeo-Christian Pabulum in the Media Research Center and Tanning Spa, so I figure, what the hell, I'll throw the lefties a crumb.

At this time, let us pause and consider what I have accomplished in my book so far, which does not yet have a title. I am still in negotiations for naming rights with several Central American nation-states, a sports hosiery company, and a Boy Scout troop, so dear reader, please be patient. So far, I have provided a thumbnail sketch of my fascinating life so that you may be drawn into the mystery and enigmatic world of Luigi Miller. I have demonstrated several examples of clever wordplay. I have illuminated the secret world of the writer by demonstrating the act of revision, so that you too, common person, can write your own book, well, at least your own postcard! I have provided Luigi Rule #1, and I have completed a summary of what I have done so far in the chapter. I did all this in less than two hours. At this rate, I shall have covered all 254 rules by tee-time after tea-time tomorrow! More cleverness, how does he do it? He, that is, I, am just warming up, baby, so hold on to your hats. In addition to the rules, I will develop a clever narrative structure which will hide the fact that I am merely a pathetic hack who is tired of substitute teaching in suburban public schools and watching *Seinfeld* reruns, who has led an extremely sheltered life, having both parents who are still alive, never auditioned for a television show, and who, in all likelihood, will never get a Ph.D.

Really, my goals for this thing are pretty meager: 1) To finish at least one goddamn thing I start; 2) to provide some diversion to myself and to my friends, who might actually think some of this is funny; 3) to let my dad know that I appreciate him waking up early on Saturday mornings to take me to some crazy swimming lesson, or creative writing class, or soccer practice; 4) to let my parents know that I appreciate them for not totally screwing me up, and that for those parts of me that are screwed up, it's not all their fault, except the lack of breast-feeding and selling me to Chilean cocaine pirates to fuel my parents' small arms smuggling trade; 5) to let my wife know that I'm glad she isn't dead, that she is a great inspiration, and that I forgive her for being such a shitty Scrabble player; 6) to thank David Eggers and James Joyce for destroying literature for us, you bastards. Now, only us differently abled, ex-Marine lesbians from Puerto Rico who single-handedly stopped Hurricane Charo from destroying Tokyo can hope to have enough chutzpah to write down a single word on a single page; and 7) to let the University of Michigan know that I forgive you guys for not giving me a diploma despite my failing nine of twelve classes I took there. And I double-forgive you for not bothering to call me up and see how I was doing. See if I stop another comet from destroying your stupid clock tower again.

I was doing counter-intelligence work for the Fjord Group in Krakow during the 1930s. Please let me be clear, the Fjord Group is an incredibly clandestine organization that bears no relationship whatsoever to a person, family, or multinational corporation whose name bears a striking similarity to the Fjord Group and would actually be spelled the same if one letter from the FJORD group were dropped. NO RELATIONSHIP WHATSOEVER. I am not just saying this to avoid being sued. It is true, there is no formal or informal agreements reached under the Geneva Convention, Article 23, Section IV, rule 31-45, which would provide for any such espionage to occur in hostile or potentially hostile countries in times of threatening or potentially threatening acts of international instability. Did I mention there is no relationship whatsoever? Not even the appearance of a relationship. There is a "J" in Fjord group—I hope you noticed that, Mr. Berg.

Anyway, I was working on an automobile assembly line in Krakow, monitoring the development of these terrible conglomerations called "unions." I am not certain that such things still exist, so let me provide a bit of historical background. Around the turn of the century, the eleventh century, that is, there was a wonderful system called "feudalism." This system was as lean and efficient as any Japanese crypto-socialist hybrid that are ever so fashionable today. All the decision-making authority, from the monetary system to rule promulgation system to the daily dress and leisure activity, was centralized in a person called a king. Kings were especially important because they were directly chosen by God. God likes certain families and hates others, so kings often were from the same family. This makes sense, as the apple does not fall far from the tree.

Let me point out an editorial change I made in the format of this novel. After an in-depth focus group and complete random poll of 2,340 American readers, I have decided to eliminate the explicit identification of the LUIGI RULES. Apparently, the poll determined 79% to 19%, 2% undecided, with a margin of error +/-2.7%, that making the LUIGI RULES so obvious was an insult to the reader's intelligence. I disagree, and I believe that one can never underestimate the brilliant ignorance of one's readers. Also, the publishers of this book thought it would be fun for me to develop a game show based on this book, in which the contestants must answer questions related to the LUIGI RULES, and if I gave them all out to everyone in a very obvious manner, it would take away some of the drama and challenge of the game show. I can't believe I used the words "drama," "challenge," and "game show" in the same sentence, but there it is. However, I will certainly find other ways to insult the reader's intelligence and manage to include the LUIGI RULES at the same time. Just as a practice, to get you in the habit of using those puny hunks of gray matter you so generously call a "brain," let me point out that there is a LUIGI RULE on this very page! Yes, that is right, this exact page you are reading now. You raced right over it without it even registering for the concise statement of moral exactitude that it is. Imbecile. To wit, "THE APPLE DOES NOT FALL FAR FROM THE TREE." You did miss it, didn't you? There, there, no sense crying about it, you'll get the hang of it one day. I believe in you. The meaning of LUIGI RULE #2 is that people are like apple trees, and that just as an apple tree produces fruit, so do people, who we call children or offspring. Good apple trees produce good fruit. Good people produce good children. All bad people come from morally deviant parents who should be herded up and imprisoned. If you are a bad person, you should obviously consider your parents to be the root of all your shortcomings and should therefore feel no remorse for whatever behavior you engage in. It's not your fault!

The assembly line is a dreary, God-awful place to work, even if one enjoys doing mind-numbing, repetitive tasks as a matter of course. I know this and fully believe that auto workers should be paid a million dollars a year (almost as much as teachers), but that is no reason for them to get all uppity and believe they have a right to, well, have rights! While this is true today, it was even more true in Krakow in 1933. These people were lucky to have jobs, let alone bitch about getting mangled in machine and working seven days a week. I can assure, Mr. Harvey Fjord was not a happy man.

I must tell you that working for Mr. Fjord was one of the most gratifying experiences of my life, even thought I am black and Jewish. I first met Mr. Fjord when I was a young Zeppelin captain in Georgia, where Mr. Fjord had a summer home. He and his lovely wife, Mrs. Harvey Fjord, came out to the country to have a ride on my dirigible. He was down to earth and affable, chatting on and on about his great love for dirigibles, and indeed aircraft in general. He told me about his vision for the future, which would be for every American citizen, to use a lightweight flying craft as a primary mode of transportation. A vision which I am proud to say came to fruition in 1974. Sadly, Mr. Fjord was not around to see this occur, well, at least not in the corporeal state in which many people knew him. I am quite confident that Mr. Fjord's humors, which were kept in a jar in the observation deck of the Fjord World Headquarters in Elkville, Michigan, bubbled and gurgled at the sight of all the little flyvers flyving about the country.

We had such a pleasant time, floating high above the red clay hills of Georgia with the clouds drifting effortlessly against the blue sky. Barely a wind blew that day. The world below seemed small and insignificant. At one point, I looked over at Mr. Fjord, who was sitting quietly by himself, staring at the farms and villages below. There was an odd expression on his face, almost melancholic.

I asked him what was the matter.

He paused for a moment and wiped a small tear from the corner of his eye. "It all goes by so damn fast, doesn't it, Luigi? So damn fast."

I didn't know what to say so I just nodded my head in agreement.

He continued, "Seeing all these farms below, it just, well, it just makes me feel a little sad. I miss it, I miss those days as a boy, growing up on the farm. It was all just so simple then. Life was simpler. You knew which way was up and who was who. I wonder sometimes if I've really accomplished anything with my life. Anything worthwhile. Have I really made life better for people with that goddamn car? I think sometimes that I really just fucked things up."

I was feeling so sorry for this guy I had to wipe away the tears that were welling in my own eyes. It really made me think, "Here is this man, the richest man in the world, who is adored by everyone everywhere, and he feels this way. He really just wanted to make things better for people, and he did, he did, but he didn't believe it himself. Maybe the rich really are just like us." I began to think of what I would say to buoy his spirits. Which Luigi Rule would I espouse to change his perception and facilitate positive thinking? I didn't have to worry about things too much though.

He pulled a metal flask from his coat jacket, threw down a shot or three and said, "Who am I kidding? I didn't fuck things up. Those goddamn Jews did, they're the ones. Well, they won't get in my way for long, will they?" With this, he threw his head back and began laughing almost uncontrollably. He then went back to where Mrs. Harvey Fjord was sitting and began kissing her on the lips. They went back into a back cabin and one can only imagine what occurred there. I was impressed by his virility, but became alarmed when I heard him shout, "Milk me, mama! Milk me like a naughty cow!"

Stephen stood for a moment, shocked. He had never read anything quite like this, and certainly not from his father. Who wrote this? For a change, he did not picture his dad as the whiskey-breath man sitting on the edge of his bed, telling him stories about dragons and pixies, nor the man who awkwardly told him about the trouble a man's penis could get him into if he were not careful. Who wrote this? Not the ashen-faced man who clutched *Ulysses* like it was a sacred text, straining to spit out each syllable in some queer race against death. This writing was strong and funny and terrible and smart. Who was this? Surely not Colin Darden, surely not Da. Stephen stood in silence. He scratched the ingrown hair on his neck and tried to name what it was he was feeling inside. He couldn't do it. Maybe that's okay too. Stephen wasn't sure exactly who this new man was, but he liked having a new memory, one that wasn't cloaked in the oppressive gray fog of grief. He felt his chest heave and his throat open, emitting a terrible moaning sound. With each breath, the emptiness that had defined his days became filled up . . . with snot and tears, with blood racing to his cheeks and his brain, and it felt good. Of course, this was not a sudden transformation, a magical lifting of the veil of sorrow, a draining of the vale of tears, a mystical purging of pain and loneliness from his heart, or some other such rubbish. It was far less than that. It was far less than anyone who has lost desires. Still, it was real, and that was something for a change.

Can you help a fellow American who's down on his luck?

Stephen pleaded with Mr. Black for the money. I am certain he did, I heard him. I was seated in the torn, leather reclining chair with my feet dangling over the edge, drinking a Diet Coke, my fourth for the morning, when Stephen made the call. Watching him pace barefoot in his blue jeans and white T-shirt across the rug, undoubtedly woven at a handloom by a thirteen-year-old Iranian girl in a small, dark factory on the outskirts of Teheran, I was struck by how confidently he carried himself. I had known him for over ten years and knew him to be poised, arrogant, self-possessed, brash, boisterous. Never was he noticeably not confident, but there was something about the way he padded across the floor, speaking into the headset, thumbing through a copy of the *Aeneid*, that I recognized the trait that separated him from me—he knew on some level that he would inevitably be successful. It was then, too, that I realized I hated him for this.

"Mr. Black, please, this is the last time, no . . . we just need a few more bucks to wrap this baby up. I swear it. No more than twenty thousand will cover it. At this point, that's nothing. Look, if we don't get it, we can't finish the picture. We still have to shoot the scenes in Ireland. Without Ireland, there's no *JJ's Eyes*. I mean, it's impossible. It's all down to Ireland, it's our ace in the hole. It's what will make this movie a cut above all the other Joyce documentaries. Of course, we'll still do the motorcycle chase scenes. I mean, you just have to, right? Am I right? But we need to do it. No, I know you're not one of the Warner brothers . . . No sir, I know that . . . Yes, I know you're just a regular guy who happened to get lucky in the stock market, yes . . . No, we do appreciate everything you've done for us. Yes, I was aware you have a son about to start college this fall and that you did not qualify for financial aid, due to money that you've saved to help care for your sick parents. Yes, I do think it is ridiculous that the government should expect you to liquidize all of your assets to pay for college before you can receive some grants for your son. I agree wholeheartedly. Yes, the government does have a vested interest in an educated work force. Wow, is it that much to go to a public university? I really had no idea. I guess I haven't been keeping up . . . I'm sure he could have gotten into an Ivy League school—no question about it . . . Speaking from experience, I think Ivy League schools might leave something to be desired, unless you're a certain type of person . . . Yes, absolutely . . . Jesus Christ—both your parents are in nursing homes? I'm so sorry, wow . . . that's tough . . . that's gotta be real hard . . . I know what caring for a sick parent is like . . . It just sort of swallows you up . . . yeah, like a fucking monsoon . . . No, I know you're not complaining—you're not a complainer— not that type of person—you've just got a lot going on right now—yes, I think I do understand what that's like. It's just . . . I know this sounds incredibly . . . incredibly . . . like Hollywood bullshit, but . . . I promised my dad on his deathbed that we would finish the film and dedicate it to him. Joyce just meant so much to him. In some ways, I think my dad's spirit is in this movie, in what we're all trying to do here. It's like I'm fulfilling a dream he had, but he was never able to go after . . . yeah, leaving Ireland to come to America, working two jobs to make ends meet, you know, the whole immigrant thing. Not an original story, I know, but I don't know, somehow since his death, the story makes more sense. It's less of a fairy tale or cliché or something . . . does any of this make any sense? I feel like I've been rambling . . . It's just, sir, the film . . ."

With this, Stephen's eyes began moistening and his voice slowed and softened as he said it, "the film." He sighed on the word "film" and somehow made it like one and a half syllables. I thought to myself, "God, this guy is good." He's a natural. They can teach you to do that stuff in acting classes. I take it back, Stephen, you deserve every fucking Kentucky Fried Chicken commercial you've got coming to you.

A moment later, he hung up the phone and wiped the corner of his eyes with his thumb and index finger. His face was pallid and his eyes red. He did not say anything, but I think we both knew then that we would not finish the film. It would take months of phone calls and e-mails and cursing and sitting in front of the computer, trying to piece together our masterpiece. Each day was more frustrating than the last as our bills grew, and our beards grew, and our bellies grew, and we realized we didn't have a good short, let alone a good feature-length, let alone anything that would be vaguely interesting to anyone beyond the walls of St. Elizabeth's.

Letter Never Sent

I wrote a letter to Stephen (since I refuse to speak to him) that we must decrease the motion in the film to increase its sense of spaciousness. Also, the verbal barrages need to be eliminated. They're just junk. Not even relentless enough for white noise. I said that until writing can develop the absence of words, writing will be inferior to music. Reading is just another form of perversity. The idea of space is always inferior to space. Begging the question, is reading silence, silence?

He wrote back that the quietest experience he had was reading *Still*, by Beckett.

"The words just roll over you, like the waves at Cape Hatteras, half asleep on the beech, ninety degrees, and you melt into the sand.

My dad almost died when he read about the revival of *Waiting for Godot* by two American comedy geniuses. 'Mork' and 'The Jerk' doing Becket, he said. The world really is coming to an end. Mere anarchy is loosed upon the world, indeed! Only in fucking America, he said. But really, who better to play alienation than an alien?" Then he laughed and turned *Jeopardy* back on.

That's how Colin was though. Indignation and a belly laugh were his twin masks, the one always lurking beneath the other.

For reasons too pathetic to mention, can you feel nostalgia for a time in your life that you once considered the most desolate and lonely, and for the environs where you experienced more failure and rejection than at any time in your life, before or since? I can, therefore I was walking along South University Street, heading towards the brick façade of the East Engineering Arch on a yellow sunshiny June day. Robins and sparrows were singing just for me, and my heart was gay.

The pleasant chit-chatting of the young co-eds making profound comments on the merits of the CIA involvement in Costa Rica, and Frisbee Golf were rudely shattered by the squeal of tires. I whipped my head around to catch a glimpse—a silver BMW convertible, bass-thumping the latest Eminem single. The driver, a pleasing young rake with raven-black hair and dark freckles, and a black, mock turtleneck top and yellow wraparound sunglasses, was forced to unceremoniously stop when a blind Chinese graduate student crossed the street against the light. I looked back at the vanity license plates, a peculiar habit of mine (Is it me or does it seem that Illinois has more vanity plates per capita than any other state?), and saw an Illinois plate that simply had the word "Black" emblazoned in the white plate.

Hopefully, you, like me, were dutifully annoyed by God's heavy-handedness here. Nothing keeps me more awake than thinking of a universe created by a god with a poor aesthetic—the god of Revelations, not the god of the Gnostic gospels. I'll probably cut this scene out of the movie version, but decided to keep it in the book version because no one is likely to make it this far into the book, or you'll probably just be skimming at this point for a sex scene or the word "penis," "vagina," or "Hot Young C**S," which were the subject line of an email I recently received. Isn't it funny that even enlightened book readers such as ourselves still fall prey to such cheap, gratuitous sex talk as is found on HORNYHOUSEWIVES.COM? I also decided to keep this scene in because it is the truth, and as an artist, I have a solemn duty to be unwavering in my obligation to present the truth, even when it is unflattering, immoral, ridiculous, or boring. It is an obligation I take very seriously. After all, I did obtain the rank of Webelos in my local scout pack, foraging onward even after my den leader demonstrated his devotion to scouting principles by hanging himself in the city jail following a drunk driving arrest.

I also pay the fines on my overdue library books.

Speaking of that, I have been so impressed by the local public libraries. The selection of books is simply average, but the clerks and librarians—I can't say enough. For example, I recently acquired $18.00 in fines, mostly due to an overdue Raffi CD, as well as a Blue's Clue's video. My two-year-old has an annoying habit of not reminding me to return the library material in a timely manner. Eileen, the lady who handled our transaction, reduced our fines to $6.00. She smiled and said that since there was no one waiting for them, there is no reason to pay the full fine. Besides, she added, "We're just happy you returned them." The thought shattered me, that someone could be so incorrigible and demonic to steal property from another, especially the local library, chilled me to my marrow. My wife says that she probably felt sorry for us, with my holey green T-Shirt, and us looking like we were wed last year at age fifteen and hanging out at the local library, not at the Border's down the street. Either way, we only paid $6.00, so I'm not going to complain.

Did I mention that Richard got his old job with the Department of Defense back? He won $4,000 in damages, and they gave him a promotion. He moved back to Virginia and is looking for a wife. He acquired a library card. I'm not sure that will help him in his quest, but the public library is a fine place to spend an afternoon, as I believe I have mentioned.

The End

We four were seated around Stephen's apartment in Boston, debating the colors of the dawning sky, which was barely visible above the tree line and rooftops of the row houses across the street. Stephen and Liz were of the opinion that pink had orange undertones. Richard posited that it was impossible and that it was all just variations of the red spectrum anyway, so we should just quit our squawking, citing an impressive knowledge of color spectrum analysis. I had a brutal sinus headache and I found the whole thing pretentious and insufferably obnoxious. I tried to close my eyes and dream of something soothing, like a cloud of acid rain to descend upon them and burn out their tongues. Richard, unable to lose an argument, was now pacing back and forth, pulling books from the bookcases and gesticulating wildly. If I were able to turn down the audio at this point, he would look something like John Cleese impersonating Hitler.

Did I forget to mention Richard's Hitler mustache? Well, it was the latest in a litany of facial hair experiments. Ever since I've known him, he's engaged in beards and mustaches of every sort and shape imaginable. From Fu Manchu to the Walrus, to the clit tickler, the loopy loop, the droopy dog, the Grizzly, the Pilgrim, the Himalayan, the Clam Sandwich, the Pie Taster, The Rubicon, the Kandahar, the Abe, the Gabe, the Aunt Mabel, the Paul of Tarsus, the Pounder, the Debutante Delite, the Mandibalian, the Corky, the Biff, the Fat Matt, the Chewy, the Chubby, the Colonel, the Burt, the Dead Mouse, the Shake, the Shaq, the Muffin Man, the Lumberger, the Stewie, the Double Dip, the Secret Handshake, the Chastity Belt, the Velvet Serpent, and now, the Hitler.

I have tried to get him to seek professional therapeutic help but I have not been successful.

He says it has nothing to do with his clean-shaven father, or the mole on his mother's left cheek, right near her lip. Having obtained a master's degree in counseling, I beg to differ with him.

Spamlet

The first film we three boys made together was in tenth grade, for extra credit in Advanced English. It was a retelling of *Hamlet*, in drag. Richard said it was to pay homage to the modern Rosencrantz and Guildensterners, Monty Python. We later came to accept that Richard enjoyed dressing up in women's clothing. To be fair, none of us complained about it too much, if you know what I am saying.

This was in 1985, and there was still something called Beta Max, the video-editing capabilities we know enjoy on our iMacs (cool product tie-in) were not in existence yet. There was also not the spate of teen Shakespeare movies that was prevalent in the 1990s. I was always hopeful to see a version of King Lear performed by students at a local elementary school. Perhaps, my next project.

That was a great film, as evidenced by the fact of winning a prize in the local community students arts contest. We won a gift certificate to the local sporting goods store, where we purchased several basketballs that we exploded for our next film that won no awards. I later sold the film to a major shoe manufacturer that they used in a promotional campaign for a basketball shoe. I received well over $500.00 for this, which I later realized was the exact amount they spent for breakfast for each day's shoot. We knew on some level that this new film was finished, but none of us really had the heart to admit it.

"We could still get money from Black, I think he's holding out on us," said Richard.

"No way, Rich. It's not going to happen, he bailed on us when we needed it most, and he's not going to come through.

He's done with us, he thinks we're a joke, and maybe he's right—this whole thing—what were we thinking?" David said.

"That's the problem right there, David. I mean, that's it exactly. You wanted this to fail from the get go," Stephen said.

"That's not true. It's not true at all. I wanted this as much as anyone else did, I'm beyond broke—I have cashed in my meager 403(b), my wife and I are being evicted, we can't pay our car payment because of this movie, and we are having a child. Do you understand that? We are having a child and I'm thirty years old, and I have $15,000 in credit card debt, and I drive a ten-year-old American car with 171,421 miles on it, and my pregnant wife and I are moving into my parents' basement because we spent all our savings, and more on this goddamn movie. So don't you dare tell me I didn't want this as much as anyone else . . . just don't you dare," David said.

"Look, none of us would have done this if we didn't want to do it, so let's just relax and enjoy our last night as film heroes," Liz said, "maybe open that Scotch you've been stashing away, Stephen . . ."

"Yeah, I suppose. It's just . . . you know, we came so close . . . maybe my dad was right . . . maybe the idea of a film about James Joyce is enough . . . maybe that's really overreaching . . ."

"A man's reach should exceed his ass," Richard added.

"Grasp," David corrected.

"A man's reach should grasp his ass," Richard said.

"You dumb shit, it's 'a man's ass should reach his grasp,'" Liz added.

"An ass by any other name . . ." David said.

"Would still be called David, the king of the shoes," Stephen said.

"On that note, I think you should open that Scotch and we can watch our movie as it was meant to be seen . . . while pissing drunk, or with eyes shut and the sound mercifully silent," Liz said, "and make mine a double, I'm drinking for two, you know."

David shot her a glance.

"A double tonic water, silly . . ." she said, laughing.

The rest of the merry band joined her gaiety and clutched each other by the arm as the scene fades to black.

Staring at Stephen's

Face, I could see his dead father. The green eyes and the rosy cheeks, and the nose that sloped gently away from the face. The waves crashing at the Isle of Skye. The gray sky that swept into eternity across the rolling green hills. The gray-haired lady in the yellow bathing suit and straw hat at Myrtle Beech, the left breast removed from cancer. The broken storefront windows, swept up achingly, lovingly by a stoop-shouldered man wearing a white apron the morning after Krystallnackt, the Detroit Riots, Bloody Sunday. Had he too not seen these with his own eyes?

I wanted to ask Stephen a million questions, about how he's doing, and is he writing and acting, and what is it like to have a dead father. It had been so long since we had sat in Richard's basement, drinking Diet Cokes, listening to *Zen Arcade* and solving the problems of the world with teenaged optimism. Most of all, I wondered if he was still an atheist, and if he was liberated because of it. What would death be like without Jesus?

But it had been so long and we had forgotten how to say such things, so we chatted feverishly about the ephemeral nature of Hollywood stardom. Sipping our decaf coffee and eating oatmeal and toast (David) and sausage and eggs (Stephen). The waitress at the diner had long since given up hopes for a speedy turnaround and had stopped even giving us dirty looks. Instead, she sat at the counter chatting absently with the sixteen-year-old bus boy about the Mustang he was going to buy once he graduated from high school.

Stephen gesticulated wildly with his fork and knife. "It's absolutely brilliant, brilliant, I tell you, David! It is the movie of the year, no—it's the movie of the decade. God, you have got to see it. It's just—it's just too . . . God, every shot, every freaking shot is like a poem, but better than a poem, it's . . . imagine if Blake had a digital camera. That's exactly what it is, all symbols and rhythm, but it's not simple, it's not obvious, it's very, very . . . Do you remember that scene in our movie, the one where Joyce is standing at the base of the Eiffel Tower? It's raining and cold and he's like stumbling around, half blind, half drunk, and he just whips it out and takes a piss, right there at the base of the Eiffel tower, and remember the camera angle we got, and how it was backlit, and it was just too perfect. That's what this movie is. It's the movie we should have made."

I chuckled, "I think we could say that to just about any movie, that it's the movie we should have made. Anyone but the one we did . . . or almost did . . . God, we should have finished it."

"We did finish it, in our own way . . ."

"In our own way, what is that supposed to mean?"

"I don't know, it just sounded good."

"Not really . . ."

"I just mean that we're unfinished sort of people."

"Like we're retarded or something?"

"No, not just that. There's people who finish things and people who do just what they need to do to get it, to understand it, and then they don't need to do it anymore. The people who finish things, they're the kind of people who are so awful because they think they have to say something, or that they have said something, like finishing the thing is so unbelievably hard or something. I mean anybody can finish something. It's the rare few that can walk away, leaving something unfinished, it's like so much more . . ."

"Lazy."

"Well, yes, lazy. Look, you sap, I'm just trying to cheer you up. Hey, when are you guys going to get the hell out of Detroit Rock City?"

"I don't know. We keep talking about it, but you know, with the baby on the way. And it's tough. Michigan pays its teachers pretty well."

"True, and you're home by three and have summers off."

I glowered at him.

"Joking. Just joking. You've got to get out of here just for a while. Take a year or two, move somewhere where you don't know anyone, and just write, for God's sake. You're a writer."

"I'm a hack."

"You're not a hack, you're awesome."

"True, I'm one of the top one thousand unpublished writers."

"You've been published."

"Great, I'm one of the bottom ten thousand published writers. When are you going back to the stage?"

"The stage, ah yes, the stage. Well, the only problem with the stage is the . . ."

"Money."

"Am I supposed to feed my soon-to-be daughter or son scripts and *Playbill* for dinner?"

"What was that movie . . ."

"*King of the Hill.* God, yes, that was intense. You know, my dad loved that movie. I think it reminded him of his own father or something."

I nodded.

Stephen was quiet for a moment, staring intently at the bottom of his empty coffee cup.

"I miss him. There's not a day goes by that I don't . . ." He didn't finish.

A man's life in less than 500 words.

Of the facts. Colin Darden was born in Belfast during the year *Ulysses* was published in the United States. He was employed as a printer, both "at home" and here in the States. He bicycled from New York to Detroit through Canada one summer in 1959. He only planned on staying in Detroit long enough to see Al Kaline play against the Yankees but was hit by an Edsel leaving the stadium, and was forced to stay in a hospital bed for six weeks. He passed the time reading James Joyce and pinching the fannies of the young candy stripers. He hated Manchester United, and knew more about U.S politics than anyone I'd met. He was the first person I'd ever met who could quote Shakespeare. He loved his garden of hyacinths and the squirrel who ate his tomatoes. He thought Pound was too tough on the Jews. Thought the Catholics were worse than the "fucking Mafia." Hated Mexican food. He wrote a letter to his mother during every one of her birthdays following her death and kept them in a cigar box on the top shelf of his bedroom closet. He returned to Belfast only once, in 1978, to bury his mother. He didn't cry at the funeral, but cried like an idiot in the bathroom stall at Billy's Pub the next day. He was reading *Ulysses* when he died of a heart attack. He lived with cancer for four years before he died, weighing ninety-four pounds at the time of his death, skin hanging in folds beneath his shoulder blades. Father of a boy and a girl. Husband.

    I visited him once before he died and he made me promise I would write about him one day in one of my stories. I told him I could never do it right. He laughed even though I could see it hurt him, his hand clutching his side. "Make sure to write down how good-looking I am."

    I told him I couldn't write about him. That I can't write about real people and that my prose was too prone to pontification, yet lacked any original insight. "I've got the ideas, but I can't ever seem to get the words right," I said.

    "Just be honest," he said, "and be yourself, for Christ's sake."

    "I'm not very good at being either."

    "That's why you're such a lousy writer," he laughed, "but you'll get it one of these days. You'll get it."

    I doubted it then, and still do. Maybe that's why it's taken us so long to get to this point. To this point: fear. The fear that, yes, there always is an ending. And it's the endings and good-byes and "fare-thee-wells" that scare me. So here it is then, a man's life in less than five hundred words. You deserved much better, but I am a coward.